I0619110

PASSPORT
TO
DANGER!

Francis Durbridge

WILLIAMS & WHITING

Copyright © Serial Productions

This edition published in 2022 by Williams & Whiting

All rights reserved

This script is fully protected under the copyright laws of the British Commonwealth of Nations, the United States of America, and all countries of the Berne and Universal Copyright Convention. All rights including Stage, Motion Picture, Radio, Television, Public Reading and the right to translate into foreign languages are strictly reserved. No part of this publication may be lawfully reproduced in any form or by any means such as photocopying, typescript, manuscript, audio or video recording or digitally or electronically or be transmitted or stored in a retrieval system without the prior written permission of the copyright owners.

Applications for performance or other rights should be made to The Agency, 24 Pottery Lane, London W11 4LZ.

The script in this book was sourced from the
BBC Written Archive Centre
and the transcriptions have been made by the publisher
and have not been checked for accuracy by the BBC.

Cover design by Timo Schroeder

Williams & Whiting (Publishers)
15 Chestnut Grove, Hurstpierpoint,
West Sussex, BN6 9SS

Titles by Francis Durbridge published by Williams & Whiting

Murder At The Weekend – the rediscovered newspaper serials and short stories

Also published by Williams & Whiting:
Francis Durbridge : The Complete Guide
By Melvyn Barnes

Titles by Francis Durbridge to be published by Williams &
Whiting
A Game of Murder
A Man Called Harry Brent
Bat Out of Hell
Breakaway – The Family Affair
Breakaway – The Local Affair
Farewell Leicester Square
Five Minute Mysteries (includes Michael Starr Investigates
and The Memoirs of Andre d'Arnell)
Johnny Washington Esquire
Melissa
Mr Hartington Died Tomorrow
Murder On The Continent (Further re-discovered serials and
stories)
One Man To Another – a novel
Operation Diplomat
Paul Temple and the Alex Affair
Paul Temple and the Canterbury Case (film script)
Paul Temple and the Conrad Case
Paul Temple and the Geneva Mystery
Paul Temple and the Gilbert Case
Paul Temple and the Gregory Affair
Paul Temple and the Jonathan Mystery
Paul Temple and the Lawrence Affair
Paul Temple and the Madison Mystery
Paul Temple and the Margo Mystery
Paul Temple and the Sullivan Mystery
Paul Temple and the Vandyke Affair

Paul Temple: Two Plays For Radio Vol 2 (Send For Paul Temple and News of Paul Temple)

Send For Paul Temple Again

The Doll

The Female of the Species (The Girl from the Hibiscus and Introducing Gail Carlton)

The Man From Washington

The Passenger

Tim Frazer and the Salinger Affair

Tim Frazer and the Mellin Forrest Mystery

INTRODUCTION

Francis Durbridge (1912-98) began his career in 1933 as a writer of sketches, stories and plays for BBC radio. They were mostly light entertainments, including libretti for musical comedies, but a talent for crime fiction became evident in his radio plays *Murder in the Midlands* (1934) and *Murder in the Embassy* (1937).

He continued to write radio plays and serials for many years, using his own name and the pseudonyms Frank Cromwell, Nicholas Vane and Lewis Middleton Harvey, but his triumph was the creation of novelist/detective Paul Temple and his wife Steve. When the serial *Send for Paul Temple* was broadcast in 1938, listeners bombarded the BBC with over 7,000 requests for more and Durbridge responded later the same year with *Paul Temple and the Front Page Men*. From 1939 to 1968 there were another twenty-six Paul Temple radio productions, of which seven were new versions of earlier cases. Then in 1952, while continuing to write for radio, Durbridge embarked on a sequence of BBC television serials (not featuring the Temples) that achieved huge viewing figures until 1980. And additionally, from 1971 in the UK and even earlier in Germany, he became known for intriguing and sophisticated stage plays.

In his career as a radio dramatist, he could have maintained his reputation simply by writing about Paul and Steve Temple. Indeed Temple stood his ground throughout the mid-twentieth century among radio detectives including Dick Barton (by Edward J. Mason), Philip Odell (by Lester Powell), Dr. Morelle (by Ernest Dudley), P.C. 49 (by Alan Stranks) and Ambrose West (by Philip Levene). But Durbridge was never buttonholed, and showed versatility on BBC radio with a range of plays, revue sketches and serials both criminous and non-criminous.

Passport to Danger! is a good example of diversification from the Paul Temple mould, being an international thriller quite different from Temple's very British cases. Broadcast from 1 August to 5 September 1945 in six thirty-minute episodes, it was produced by Vernon Harris – a significant change, as Martyn C. Webster was Durbridge's regular producer. From correspondence in the BBC Written Archives Centre it appears that Durbridge originally planned to call this serial *And This Is Stephen Lewis*, but he obviously changed his mind because no Stephen Lewis appears in the script. No information about the plot was published in the *Radio Times*, which means that now – almost eighty years later – we can finally learn what this was all about.

Carl Bernard (as Tim Valentine) would in today's parlance be described as a shoe-in because he earlier appeared as Paul Temple in the one-hour abridged production of the original *Send for Paul Temple* in 1941, as Johnny Cordell in *The Man from Washington* in 1941, as Hugo Bismarck in Durbridge's pseudonymous television works *The Girl at the Hibiscus* and *Death Comes to the Hibiscus* in 1941, and as Temple again in *Paul Temple Intervenes* in 1942. His co-star, Linden Travers, was predominantly a film actress (with many credits including Hitchcock's *The Lady Vanishes* in 1938), but she made occasional radio appearances. In fact, before *Passport to Danger!* she had already co-starred with Kenneth Kent in Durbridge's nine episodes of "weekly detective problems" called *The Memoirs of André d'Arnell* that were broadcast weekly in *Monday Night at Eight* (9 October to 27 November 1944 and 18 December 1944).

In *Passport to Danger'* there were other actors who regularly enhanced radio productions over the years - including Wilfred Babbage, Phillip Leaver, Ian Sadler, Stephen Jack and Andrea Malandrinos. And there was the almost inevitable Marjorie Westbury, who had appeared on

BBC radio as an actress and singer in Durbridge plays from the early 1930s and in *Paul Temple Intervenes* (the small role of Dolly Fraser) in 1942. She went on to make Steve Temple her own in *Send for Paul Temple Again* (1945) for the first of twenty-two occasions until the final serial *Paul Temple and the Alex Affair* (1968). In the process she partnered Kim Peacock and Peter Coke in all their appearances (1946-68), and before Peacock she had played Steve opposite Barry Morse in *Send for Paul Temple Again* (1945) and Howard Marion-Crawford in *A Case for Paul Temple* (1946).

The radio exploits of Paul Temple built an impressive UK and European fanbase, leading to four cinema movies and numerous novels and becoming a brand spawning a syndicated newspaper strip from December 1950 to May 1971 and a television series from 1969 to 1971 (although this was not written by Durbridge). And on the Continent, Paul Temple radio serials were broadcast in translation and using their own actors from 1939 in the Netherlands, 1949 in Germany, 1953 in Italy and 1954 in Denmark. But Durbridge's non-Temple thrillers appear to have been less popular abroad, with *Passport to Danger!* waiting until 1985 when the Dutch broadcaster AVRO produced their version in six episodes from 8 October 1985, entitled *Een reis vol gevaren*, translated by J.C. van der Horst and produced by Hero Muller, with Manfred de Graaf as Tim Valentine and Barbara Hoffmann as Linda West.

Durbridge's non-Temple radio plays and serials have largely been forgotten, which makes this series of published scripts such a fascinating revelation. Until now his name has been synonymous with Temple, particularly given the added fillip when from 2006 to 2013 the BBC took surviving radio scripts and re-created the serials with new actors and traditional sound effects. The first of these, *Paul Temple and the Sullivan Mystery* (from 1948), was followed by *Paul*

Temple and the Madison Mystery (from 1949), *Paul Temple and Steve* (from 1947), *A Case for Paul Temple* (from 1946) and *Paul Temple and the Gregory Affair* (from 1946) – all produced by Patrick Rayner, breathing new life into these thrillers for an audience that had not heard the originals.

Passport to Danger! has never been repeated on the radio nor reproduced in any other form, which makes this volume a unique achievement.

Melvyn Barnes
Author of *Francis Durbridge The Complete Guide* (Williams & Whiting, 2018)

This book reproduces Francis Durbridge's original script together with the list of characters and actors of the BBC programme on the dates mentioned, but the eventual broadcast might have edited Durbridge's script in respect of scenes, dialogue and character names.

PASSPORT TO DANGER!

A serial in six episodes

By FRANCIS DURBRIDGE

Broadcast on BBC Radio

1 August – 5 September 1945

CAST:

Linda West	Linden Travers
Tim Valentine	Carl Bernard
Philip Millais	Phillip Leaver
Norman Staines	Carleton Hobbs
Mike	Ian Sadler
Major Hadley	Norman Shelley
Rita	Edna Kaye
Mrs Penelope	Joan Young
Maria	Olwen Brooks
Ryder	Basil Jones
Steward	Basil Jones
Don Quisando	Ian Sadler
Guiseppe	Jacques Brown
Singer	Edna Kaye
Tinker-Bell Smith	Stephen Jack
Nicky Dimitros	Andrea Melandrinos
Ruby Thompson	Dorothy Carless
Peter Vandare	Finlay Currie
	And MacDonald Parke
Carlos	Stephen Jack
Roger Knight	Wilfred Babbage
Mrs Tressburg	Gladys Young
Jacques	George Owen
Dumas	Stephen Jack

Nurse . . . . Gladys Young
Renee . . . . Michele de Lys
Announcer . . . . Norman Wooland
Music by Hal Evans played by The Dance Orchestra
Conductor: Stanley Black

EPISODE ONE

IN WHICH
A YOUNG LADY
SAYS "YES"

OPEN to the background noises of a small – not overcrowded night club. Music can be heard.

MILLAIS: (*With authority*) Luigi!

LUIGI: (*At once*) Monsieur?

MILLAIS: I'm expecting Mr Ryder. As soon as he arrives show him straight to my table.

LUIGI: Certainly, sir. (*Smiling, confidentially*) Rita is with us again tonight, sir.

MILLAIS: Oh, is she! Then ask the little devil to sing that song for me!

MILLAIS: (*Laughing*) Certainly, sir! (*Suddenly*) Ah, here's Mr Ryder! (*Pleasantly*) Good evening, sir!

RYDER: Evening, Luigi! Hello, Philip!

MILLAIS: Sit down.

RYDER: Thanks.

MILLAIS: (*After a moment*) Well? You look very pleased with yourself.

RYDER: I feel very pleased with myself. I've got some news for you.

MILLAIS: Yes. I've got some news for you too, my friend.

RYDER: I think you'll find my news rather – to say the least, Philip – surprising.

MILLAIS: With all due modesty I don't think mine will pass entirely unnoticed. However, go on, my friend ...

The music finishes and there is a smattering of applause.

RYDER: (*Lowering his voice*) Listen! You wanted me to get rid of the West girl for you, didn't you? Linda West – the actress ...

MILLAIS: (*Quietly, seriously*) Well?

RYDER: (*After a moment – tensely*) She's dead. They picked her out of the Thames – just over an hour ago!

3

Quick FADE UP of an introductory roll on the drums followed by slight applause.

RYDER: Philip ...

MILLAIS: Quiet.

RITA and the Orchestra perform Can This Be You at the end of which there is applause. Music then continues under the following dialogue.

MILLAIS: I think that girl gets better every time she sings!

RYDER: Philip, you heard what I said – about – Linda West?

MILLAIS: Yes, I heard.

RYDER: You don't seem very surprised.

MILLAIS: No. No, I'm not surprised, my friend. You see, I happen to know that Linda West was not picked out of the river tonight. She appeared – as usual – at the Commodore Theatre.

RYDER: (*Stunned*) What do you mean?

MILLAIS: To be brief, my friend – you've murdered the wrong girl!

RITA starts to sing again. Her voice fades out at the end of the song. FADE UP the orchestra to full.

FADE DOWN the music on the last note.

LINDA: Well – thank goodness for that – no more greasepaint for a fortnight, Freda.

FREDA: It ought to be three months. You're not rehearsing tomorrow are you, Miss Linda?

LINDA: Not till the afternoon.

There is a tap on the door.

LINDA: No one tonight, Freda. Unless it's ...

FREDA: (*Going to the door*) You leave it to me.

The door opens.

STAINES: May I come in?

FREDA: Oh – it's Mr Staines.

4

LINDA: Why, hello, Norman! Yes, of course, come in.

STAINES: (*Coming in*) Are you feeling any better, Linda?

LINDA: Yes. Yes, I'm all right now, darling. But I'm most terribly sorry.

The door closes.

STAINES: (*Quietly*) You had me quite worried, Linda – nearly passing out like that in the middle of a big scene.

LINDA: (*With a little laugh*) Yes, still ... it's all over now, Norman. Six hundred performances!

STAINES: Thanks to you, Linda.

LINDA: Nonsense! The dialogue was charming and the story – well the story always was a pretty good one.

STAINES laughs.

LINDA: I knew it was going to be a winner, Norman – right from the beginning.

STAINES: Yes. Yes, I believe you did. (*A moment's hesitation*) Linda, we've known each other a very long time – haven't we?

LINDA: A <u>very</u> long time, Norman. Do you remember that morning – in the old office in the Waterloo Road?

STAINES: (*Laughing*) A little girl with pigtails reciting The Charge of the Light Brigade. Yes – yes, I remember. You recited it very badly, by the way – I've always wanted to tell you that.

LINDA: (*Laughing, but strangely near to tears*) Yes ... Yes, I know.

STAINES: (*Quietly*) What is it, Linda?

LINDA: Nothing, Norman. I'm all right –

STAINES: (*After a moment*) What is it, Linda?

LINDA: Darling, I've told you – nothing. I'm just a little depressed because the show's finished – that's all.

STAINES: (*Quietly*) Is that why you nearly fainted?

LINDA: (Quietly, tensely) Norman, please, I've told you I … I … (*She breaks off*)

STAINES: It's no use pretending. For weeks now you've been worried, desperately worried. I've watched you, Linda. I've watched you in your dressing room before the show; in restaurants; in hotels; at rehearsals; I've watched you at odd little moments when – when you've been off your guard. (*A moment*) What is it, Linda? What's the matter?

LINDA: (*Suddenly*) Oh – I've been so miserable! I haven't known which way to turn. (*A note of desperation*) Norman, I've got to talk to you! I've got to tell someone about it or I shall go crazy!

STAINES: (*Quietly, curious*) Is it about – your brother?

LINDA: (*Surprised*) Why – why, yes! How did you know?

STAINES: You haven't mentioned him recently – not for some months in fact. At one time, you know, you always used to be talking about him.

LINDA: Roger was working on a provincial paper. Then suddenly he had a lucky break and landed a job as Foreign Correspondent on The Daily Graphic. When he came to Town he changed his name to Roger Knight – and …

STAINES: (*Astonished*) Roger Knight! I never knew your brother was Roger Knight! Why I used to read his articles regularly – almost every week.

LINDA: (*Quietly, with a serious undertone*) Yes …

6

STAINES: (*Quietly, interested*) Go on, Linda.

LINDA: After he'd been in Town for two or three weeks the paper sent him out to North Africa – and then later to the Isle of Marapest. (*A moment*) I had one note from Marapest, Norman. Rather – rather an extraordinary note.

STAINES: What do you mean?

LINDA: Well – Roger said that he's discovered something – something pretty big – and that in a week or two he'd send me all the details. He said that he'd like me to hear all about it from himself, personally, rather than just read it in the newspapers.

STAINES: What was he referring to?

LINDA: I don't know. That was four months ago. I haven't heard a word since.

STAINES: Four months ago! But – but what's happened? (*Puzzled*) What's happened?

LINDA: He's – he's disappeared ...

STAINES: Disappeared? (*A little laugh*) What do you mean ...

LINDA: For four months now, we've heard nothing from him – no letters, no articles, no communication of any sort. The Graphic sent a man out to investigate – he reported that – Roger had simply – disappeared.

STAINES: But that's nonsense! He can't just have vanished into thin air. Why?

LINDA: (*Tensely, slowly*) I don't know. If you ask me, there's something queer going on – something queer about the whole business. The newspaper haven't even mentioned his name, and when I tried to – to –

7

STAINES: (*Pleasantly*) Now, Linda, don't be stupid. I'm sure …

LINDA: (*Overwrought*) Something's happened to him, Norman! I feel it! I feel distinctively that …

STAINES: Now, listen, Linda! These Foreign Correspondents are always disappearing. It's part of their stock-in-trade. You can see what's happened. He's stumbled on to something pretty big and he doesn't want anyone else to know anything about it. (*Quietly*) He'll turn up all right, Linda, I feel sure of it.

LINDA: (*Softly, tensely*) I hope you're right, Norman. I do hope you're right.

There is a tap on the door. The door opens.

FREDA: It's Mike, Miss Linda.

STAINES: (*Pleasantly*) Hello, Mike!

MIKE: Good evening, sir. The car's ready, Miss West.

LINDA: Thanks, Mike. I'm just ready.

MIKE: I trust you're feeling more yourself now, ma'am?

LINDA: Yes, I'm feeling much better now, Mike – thank you. Pass me that wrap, Freda. No, don't trouble to come down, Norman darling – I'm all right.

STAINES: Well, remember what I've told you. There's nothing to worry about – I feel sure of it.

LINDA: You've been a dear! I'll see you tomorrow at rehearsal.

STAINES: Goodnight, Linda. God bless!

FADE DOWN on last words of above.

FADE IN a car travelling at about thirty miles an hour.

LINDA: Did you see the show tonight, Mike?

MIKE: I did that. And when you nearly passed out, why – why you could have bowled me over with a feather.

LINDA:	(*A little laugh*) I'll bet you could.
MIKE:	Still, you acted everyone else off the stage. And you looked just like a picture.
LINDA:	A very nice picture, I hope, Mike.
MIKE:	'Tis the Mona Lisa I have in mind.

LINDA laughs.

MIKE:	And how's the new show going now?
LINDA:	The rehearsals seem to be going quite well, Mike. (*With a laugh*) Although Mr Staines seems to think we're in for a flop.
MIKE:	Ah! You must be taking no notice of that, for if ever a man invited trouble I'm thinking it's Mr … (*He breaks off*)
LINDA:	(*Softly, alarmed*) What is it, Mike?
MIKE:	(*Slowly, bewildered*) There seems to be something the matter with the steering wheel. Why the blessed thing won't … won't …
LINDA:	(*Suddenly, desperately*) Mike!!!
MIKE:	(*Quickly, shouting*) Look out!!!

LINDA screams.
There is a crash as the car rides on the pavement, a screeching of brakes, and a sudden volley of sound as the car smashes headlong into a shop window.
Music starts – full up immediately following the crash –
FADE DOWN on last notes.

LINDA:	(*Weakly, frightened and confused*) Where am I? What's happened? Mike! Mike! Did – did I faint – or – or –
TIM:	Take it easy, lady! You'll be o.k.
MIKE:	(*Nervously*) Is – is she going to be all right, sir?
TIM:	Sure. She's only passed out. I say, you'd better get that hand of yours seen to – it doesn't look too

9

	good to me! Ah! Here we are! (*Pleasantly*) Feeling better?
LINDA:	(*Still dazed*) Yes, I … (*Suddenly*) Mike! Mike, did I – faint again?
TIM:	Again? Is this a habit of yours?
LINDA:	Why – where – where am I? Whose car is this?
MIKE:	It's this gentleman's, ma'am – he saw the crash, and …
TIM:	Dragged you out of the blazing wreckage. It was most impressive.
LINDA:	Well .. I …
TIM:	Take it easy, now.
LINDA:	This seems to be quite a night! I'm very grateful to you, Mr –?
TIM:	Valentine.
LINDA:	Mr Valentine.
TIM:	Not at all.
LINDA:	But … I'm still a little concerned – I mean – well – what exactly happened?
MIKE:	Well, I don't rightly know what happened, ma'am! We were sailing along – peacefully like, as you might say – when suddenly the steering wheel went 'phut'.
TIM:	One minute you were on the road – the next you seemed to be heading straight for the shop window.
MIKE:	I tugged at the wheel, sir, but nothing happened. Not a blaming thing.
TIM:	Extraordinary! Perfectly extraordinary!
MIKE:	I'm sorry, Miss West, but for the life of me now I don't see what else I could …
LINDA:	Oh, that's all … (*Suddenly*) Oh! Look at your hand, Mike!

10

MIKE: Ah, 'tis nothing – only a scratch. (*Grieved*) But I'm afraid the car's in a pretty bad way.

TIM: To say nothing of the shop window.

LINDA: Don't worry about the car, Mike!

MIKE: Well, I'm thinking you'll be needing a taxi now, ma'am, so if you'll …

TIM: Taxi? What's the matter with my old crate?

LINDA: No, really, I …

TIM: Don't be silly. I'll drive you home with pleasure. How far are you going?

LINDA: Brook Street.

TIM: Brook Street? Easy! (*Curiously*) By the way, aren't you Linda West – Linda West, the actress?

LINDA: Yes.

TIM: (*A little laugh*) Ah! Thought so! (*For some unaccountable reason he is highly amused*) Extraordinary! Perfectly extraordinary! (*He continues to laugh*)

FADE OUT.

FADE IN a lift ascending. It stops. The lift gates open.

LINDA: Here we are.

TIM: Where to now?

The lift gates close.

LINDA: It's the door on the left! Now where did I put that key? I'm sure I … Ah!

LINDA puts the key in the lock. The door opens.

MARIA: Good evening, Miss Linda!

LINDA: (*Surprised*) Oh, hello, Maria.

The door closes.

LINDA: I thought you'd be in bed by now.

MARIA: I just go.

LINDA: (*Pleasantly*) You should have been in bed hours ago.

11

MARIA: (*Sleepily*) I haf been reading this book an' fall asleep.

TIM: (*Reading the title of the book*) The Unbridled Passion by Rosie Granger. No wonder you fell asleep!

MARIA: Ja! It stinks!

LINDA: (*Laughing*) I've told you not to use that word. (*Casually*) Do help yourself to a drink, Mr Valentine.

TIM: (*Hesitating*) Well, I suppose I really ought to be going. I've an appointment at ... (*Suddenly impressed*) My! My! You seem to have pretty well everything here. Whisky – sherry – brandy – gin – French – Italian vermouth – I say! I say!! I say!!!

LINDA: (*Laughing*) I'll have a glass of milk, Maria.

MARIA: (*Wearily*) Ja! See! It is ready – on the small table.

LINDA: Oh, yes.

MARIA: Oh! There was a telephone call for you. Four times there was a telephone call.

LINDA: Oh?

MARIA: I wrote the name down. A – Major Hadley.

LINDA: (*Puzzled*) Major Hadley? Are you sure you got the name right?

MARIA: Ja! Four times he telephone – four times I write down the name. See! Hadley ... H-a-d-l-e-y.

LINDA: Did he say what he wanted – this – Major Hadley?

MARIA: No. No. I say you not in – he say, t'ank you very much I ring again. Four times he ring.

LINDA: I see. Thank you, Maria.

MARIA: Goodnight.

LINDA: Goodnight.

The door opens and closes.

TIM: Well, I've taken you at your word and helped myself.

LINDA:	M'm? Oh – good.
TIM:	Down the hatch!
LINDA:	Cheerio!
TIM:	(*After a moment*) Are you sure you're quite happy with that glass of milk?
LINDA:	Quite sure.
TIM:	Well, you know best. (*Pleasantly*) I take it you feel all right now? No quaking at the knees, or quickening of the pulse?
LINDA:	(*Laughing*) No. (*Puzzled*) But you know, I really can't understand it. I mean, as a rule, Mike's such a careful driver.
TIM:	Well – he's certainly a very lucky one!
LINDA:	It's a good thing for us you happened to be passing – I'm really awfully grateful to you.
TIM:	Nonsense! Damsels in distress are our speciality. Ask any newspaper man.
LINDA:	(*Faintly surprised*) Are you a – newspaper man?
TIM:	Yes, I'm on The London Tribune.
LINDA:	Oh the – (*Suddenly*) I say, you're not Timothy Valentine by any chance?
TIM:	Yes.
LINDA:	Not – not the Timothy Valentine the Foreign Correspondent?
TIM:	Yes; I'm – rather afraid I am.
LINDA:	Good gracious! This is really extraordinary! I mean – well – I've heard such a lot about you that …
TIM:	(*Glibly*) I've heard a lot about you, too.
LINDA:	Yes, I know, but – (*With a little laugh*) as a matter of fact I've only just finished reading a book of yours.
TIM:	Europe Inside Out?
LINDA:	Yes.

13

TIM: I bet you didn't buy a copy!

LINDA: (*Laughing*) No, I'm afraid I didn't. I …

TIM: Borrowed it from a friend – yes – yes, I know!
          (*They laugh; suddenly*) Ah, well – I must be off!
          Thanks for the drink.

LINDA: (*Hesitantly*) Mr Valentine …

TIM: Yes?

LINDA: Do you – do you by any chance happen to know –
          Roger Knight?

TIM: Roger Knight? Why, yes, of course! He's my
          counterpart on The Daily Graphic. Quite a boy! (*A
          moment – curious*) Why do you ask?

LINDA: (*Vaguely*) Oh – I used to read his articles – that's
          all. He doesn't seem to write anything these days –
          does he?

TIM: (*Quietly, his thoughts elsewhere*) Doesn't he? (*A
          moment, curiously*) Miss West, that accident
          tonight seemed to me to be, well … (*Hesitantly*)
          Well, I was just thinking, if anything like that
          happens again – which it won't of course – but …

LINDA: (*Quietly*) If anything like that happens again?

TIM: (*Seriously*) Well, I'd like you to know that you can
          always – always rely on me.

LINDA: (*Softly*) Thank you.

TIM: (*Suddenly, lightly*) In a completely reliable sort of
          way I'm very reliable.

LINDA laughs.

The door buzzer sounds.

LINDA: (*Faintly surprised*) Hello! I wonder if that's Mike
          …

The door opens.

MIKE: (*Coming in – excitedly*) I beg your pardon, Miss
          West, but could I have a word with you?

LINDA: Why, yes, certainly, Mike. Come in.

TIM: (*Pleasantly*) Are you feeling ok, now?

MIKE: Yes. Yes, I'm fine, thank you, sir. But t'was a mighty narrow shave I'm thinking.

TIM: I'm thinking it was. Well – goodnight. (*Going*) Keep your fingers crossed!

LINDA: (*Laughing*) Goodnight.

The door closes.

MIKE: I'm sorry bursting in on you like this, ma'am, but …

LINDA: Well? What is it, Mike?

MIKE: (*Seriously*) It's the car, Miss. I'm just a little in the way of being perplexed, as you might say.

LINDA: Perplexed?

MIKE: (*Hesitantly*) Well, beggin' your pardon, ma'am, but in a manner o' speaking, the accident tonight wasn't – exactly – an accident.

LINDA: What do you mean?

MIKE: I've examined the car and the draglink had been forced out of its socket. It was held together by a piece of wire. Sooner or later, of course, the wire was bound to give way an' the steering go to pieces. (*Ominously*) That's exactly what happened tonight, ma'am.

LINDA: (*Quietly, staggered*) Mike, are you trying to tell me that the car had been tampered with? That someone quite deliberately went out of their way to …

MIKE: (*Grimly*) Yes, ma'am.

LINDA: (*Laughing*) Oh, but that's preposterous!

MIKE: (*Dogmatically*) Well, that's how I see things, Miss West. (*Suddenly*) Here! Here's the piece of wire – you can see for yourself – it's quite new.

15

LINDA: (*Quietly*) Yes. (*A pause*) Let someone else take a look at the car tomorrow morning – someone you know.

MIKE: (*Going*) Yes. Yes, all right, ma'am.

The door opens.

MIKE: Goodnight, and I'm sorry to have troubled you.

The phone starts ringing.

LINDA: (*Thoughtfully, worried*) No. No, I'm glad you called. Goodnight, Mike.

The door closes.

After a moment, LINDA lifts the telephone receiver.

LINDA: (*Her thoughts elsewhere*) Hello?

HADLEY: Hello? Who is that, please?

LINDA: This is Mayfair 9998.

HADLEY: Miss West?

LINDA: (*Tentatively*) Yes, this is Miss West speaking.

HADLEY: (*Pleasantly*) Oh, good evening, Miss West. I tried to get you earlier in the evening but your maid said you were out. My name is Major Hadley.

LINDA: (*Suddenly – remembering*) Oh, yes!

HADLEY: Forgive me telephoning you at this unearthly hour but the matter is, I assure you, of some importance.

LINDA: I – I don't think we've met, Major Hadley?

HADLEY: No, but I trust that oversight will very soon be rectified.

LINDA: (*Rather coldly*) What is it you wish to speak to me about?

HADLEY: (*Very sure of himself*) I should like to see you, Miss West. Shall we say tomorrow afternoon at three o'clock. The address is 49a Half Moon Street.

LINDA: That's quite out of the question! I have a rehearsal at three and besides …

16

HADLEY: The matter is, I assure you, of some importance.

LINDA: (*Annoyed*) Look here! You can hardly expect me to keep an appointment with someone I've never even seen, let alone ...

HADLEY: (*Interrupting LINDA – quite determined*) Miss West – the matter is, I assure you, of some importance. Make a note of the address please, 49a Half Moon Street ... (*Politely*) At three o'clock. Goodbye. (*He rings off*)

Music sounds.

LINDA: (*Confused and indignant*) Yes, but ... look here! You simply can't just ring up on the telephone and expect ... Hello! Hello!

The receiver is rattled impatiently.

LINDA: Operator! Operator! Hello!!

CROSS FADE on the last words with music coming up to full.

FADE DOWN on the last notes of the music.

A door opens.

JUDY: Miss West, sir.

HADLEY: Thank you, Judy. And – er – for the next five minutes or so I don't wish to be disturbed.

JUDY: No, sir.

The door closes.

HADLEY: Sit down, Miss West, please.

The telephone receiver is lifted.

HADLEY: Operator, I don't want any more calls through here – not for five or ten minutes ... No, I'll ring you myself ... Thank you.

The receiver is replaced.

HADLEY: Now, Miss West, I believe that you've already spoken to Divisional-Inspector Banks and Superintendent Hutchinson of Scotland Yard ...

17

LINDA: (*Irritatedly*) Yes, after your somewhat unorthodox telephone message last night …

HADLEY: (*Chuckling*) Decided to check up on me? I trust that you were satisfied?

LINDA: (*Coldly*) Major Hadley, what is it you want?

HADLEY: I thought I'd explained that to you over the telephone?

LINDA: (*Slowly*) You said you wanted to see me on a matter of some importance.

HADLEY: Yes.

LINDA: Well – I'll give you exactly five minutes.

HADLEY: My word, you are an impetuous young lady! Not in the least what I expected.

LINDA: I'm sorry to disappoint you.

HADLEY: Oh, I'm not disappointed. Not yet. However, five minutes should be ample, providing you have the good sense not to interrupt me. (*A slight pause*) You will observe that it is now – by my wristlet watch – precisely four-fifteen.

LINDA: (*Suddenly, aghast*) Where – where did you get that watch?

HADLEY: (*Politely – faintly amused*) You find it interesting?

LINDA: (*Tensely*) Where did you get it?

HADLEY: (*Quietly*) It was sent to us from Marapest by a man called Peter Vandare. (*Politely*) You recognise the watch, Miss West?

LINDA: (*Excited, unable to control herself*) Yes! It's my brother's! I swear it! It belongs to my brother! Why I'd know … (*Quietly, yet tensely*) Major Hadley, have you any news of Roger? Have you heard from him – recently, I mean?

HADLEY: Unfortunately, no, but … (*Quietly*) Supposing you sit down for a moment or two and listen to what I've got to say. (*A moment*) Four months ago your

18

brother was appointed Foreign Correspondent to The Daily Graphic. He was sent out to Africa and then later transferred to the Isle of Marapest. He'd been in Marapest for precisely two weeks when he suddenly took it into his head to contact a man called Peter Vandare. Vandare is a Canadian and is attached to what is known as K.9 …

LINDA: (*Puzzled*) K.9? What is that?

HADLEY: Well – its an off-shoot of D.4. but is chiefly concerned with non-military affairs. (*Smiling*) To simplify matters shall we simply say British Intelligence Service?

LINDA: (*Astonished*) Is my brother a member of the British Intelligence?

HADLEY: No, but he had a pretty shrewd suspicion that Vandare was, that's why he contacted him and handed over the watch. Vandare sent the watch to London. We examined it and discovered that a message has been scrawled, rather crudely I regret to say, on the inside of the strap.

LINDA: What is the message?

HADLEY: (*A moment's pause*) Read it for yourself.

LINDA: (*After a moment – reading*) Not far from Oran there is a place called Ras-el-Ma. (*Bewildered*) What does that mean?

HADLEY: We don't know – yet.

LINDA: (*Slowly*) Not far from Oran there is a place called Ras-el-Ma. (*Quietly*) Major Hadley, ever since my brother disappeared I've been making enquiries about him. I've been everywhere. Scotland Yard – The Foreign Office – The Home Office. But I've found out precisely nothing.

HADLEY: Well?

19

LINDA: Well – why have you suddenly changed your mind? Why are you telling me all this?

HADLEY: Your brother – rightly or wrongly – decided to play a lone game. Except for the completely unintelligible message on the wristlet watch he never even contacted me.

LINDA: Well?

HADLEY: (*Quite simply*) Well – how would you like to go to Marapest, Miss West? How would you like to try and find out exactly what it was your brother discovered?

LINDA: (*Quietly, astonished*) What do you mean?

HADLEY: (*Slowly*) I mean – how would you like to try and find Roger Knight?

LINDA: (*Stunned*) Are you serious?

HADLEY: Perfectly serious.

LINDA: But – but I'm rehearsing a new play. I'm under contract to Mr Staines and – and – when would you want me to leave?

HADLEY: There's a plane leaving for Casablanca tomorrow morning.

LINDA: Tomorrow morning? (*A nervous little laugh*) Why that's – that's quite out of the question. I – I ... (*She hesitates – curious*) Could everything be arranged by tomorrow morning?

HADLEY: What do you mean?

LINDA: Well, for one thing, my passport expired on ...

HADLEY: (*Interrupting LINDA*) Your passport expired on October 22nd, 1939. But everything is quite in order, Miss West – I've seen to that. You've simply got to make up your mind – you've simply got to say 'yes' or 'no'.

LINDA: (*Suddenly – desperately*) Yes. Yes, I'll go! I'll go! I'll talk to Norman about the play tonight. Whatever happens I've got to find Roger!

HADLEY: Good. But, please, have no illusions. Remember – this is a Passport to Danger!

MUSIC starts – full up.

CROSS FADE with the sound of an approaching car. The car arrives. The sound of brakes, the car door opens.

The sound of footsteps. A knock is heard and then after a moment the door is unlatched and opened.

MILLAIS: You're late, my friend!

RYDER: (*Nervously*) Yes, you see I didn't know …

MILLAIS: Come inside! We can't talk here!

The door closes.

RYDER: Philip, what is it? What do you want?

MILLAIS: (*Slowly, watching RYDER*) Don't you know what I want?

RYDER: Philip, why did you send for me like this? I was out of town when your telegram came and …

MILLAIS: I sent for you, my dear Ryder, because – because I have an extremely generous disposition. (Sharply) To be brief: I'm going to give you just one more chance!

RYDER: One more chance?

MILLAIS: Yes, and let us hope that this time – the third time – you will be more fortunate.

RYDER: (*Tensely, quickly*) Philip, I couldn't help it! I – I did my damnedest with the car! It was almost a miracle how she escaped. Why …

MILLAIS: I'm not interested in miracles, I'm interested in one thing only, my friend! I want Miss Linda West out of the way!

21

RYDER:	(*With a nervous little laugh*) Well, I'm afraid from now on old boy – you'll have to do your own dirty work.
MILLAIS:	What do you mean?
RYDER:	Linda West leaves tomorrow morning for – Casablanca.
MILLAIS:	(*Astounded*) Are you sure?
RYDER:	Of course I'm sure!
MILLAIS:	(*Suddenly, threatening RYDER*) Ryder, listen! If this is true, there's something you've got to do for me. I don't care how you do it! But do it!
RYDER:	(*Frightened*) Do what?
MILLAIS:	Get me a seat on that plane … Get me a seat on that plane to Casablanca!

MUSIC starts.

CROSSFADE Music to a four-engine plane ticking over.

STEWARD:	Name please.
MRS P:	(*Coming in – breathlessly*) My name is Penelope. Mrs Penelope. I reserved accommodation – or should one call it accommodation – late last night and …
STEWARD:	Yes, madam. Number nine on the right.
MRS P:	(*Going*) Oh, oh, thank you. Thank you very much.
STEWARD:	Name please?
LINDA:	Miss West.
STEWARD:	Oh, yes, Miss Linda West. Number four – on the left.
LINDA:	Thank you.
TIM:	(*A little away – pleasantly*) Hello!
LINDA:	(*Astonished*) Why, hello! I didn't expect to see you again!

TIM:	(*Coming in*) Well, if it comes to that I didn't expect to see you either. (*Curious*) Where are you off to?
LINDA:	I'm – I'm going abroad.
TIM:	(*Moving away*) So am I! Extraordinary! How perfectly extraordinary!
STEWARD:	Good morning, sir.
MILLAIS:	My name is Millais – Philip Millais.
STEWARD:	(*Studying his list*) Mill – sir … Oh, yes, Mr Millais. Number seven, on the left, sir. You can leave the large case here, sir.
MILLAIS:	Thank you.
STEWARD:	I'll bring your case along, sir. This way.
TIM:	Let me put that bag on the rack for you, madam.
MRS P:	Oh, thank you. Thank you. That's really most awfully kind of you. (*Pleasantly*) My name is Penelope. Mrs Violet Penelope.
TIM:	(*Introducing himself*) Timothy Valentine – and this is Miss West.
MRS P:	Oh, how do you do, my dear?
LINDA:	How do you do?
MILLAIS:	(*After a moment's pause – calling*) Steward!
STEWARD:	(*Coming*) Yes, Mr Millais?
MILLAIS:	Would you be good enough to get me a drink, please?
STEWARD:	Certainly, sir. What would you like, sir?
MILLAIS:	A ginger ale.
STEWARD:	Very good, sir.
TIM:	(*After a moment*) Are you going far, Mrs Penelope?
MRS P:	Well, I'm flying to Casablanca and then continuing my journey by train. (*Vaguely*) My destination is … Oran.

23

Music starts.

LINDA: Oran?

MRS P: Yes. Have you ever been to Oran, Miss West?

LINDA: No, I'm afraid I haven't.

MRS P: Oh, charming spot. Really delightful. So colourful – so quaint – so – so fascinating. (*A moment – almost a wistful afterthought*) Not far from Oran there is a place called Ras-el-Ma.

FADE UP music.

END OF EPISODE ONE

EPISODE TWO

IN WHICH WE MEET
DON QUISANDO

ANNOUNCER: During a visit to the Isle of Marapest, Roger Knight, Foreign Correspondent of The Daily Graphic, has mysteriously disappeared. His sister – Linda West, the well-known actress – is invited by the British Authorities to fly to Marapest to try to find him. Prior to Linda's departure however, a message has been received, purported to come from Roger, which reads: (*Quietly*) "Not far from Oran there is a place called Ras-el-Ma". When Linda takes her seat on the plane she discovers, to her astonishment, that Tim Valentine, a recent acquaintance of hers, is to be a fellow passenger.

Music starts.

ANNOUNCER: Also on the plane are Mrs Violet Penelope and a mysterious gentleman by the name of Philip Millais.

FADE IN the sound of an air-liner engine ticking over.

ANNOUNCER: (*Authoritatively*) We are in the plane about to start for Casablanca en route to – Marapest!

CROSS FADE music out and the plane engines up.

TIM: Let me take your case for you – I'll put it on the rack.

MRS P: Oh, thank you. Thank you. That's really most awfully kind of you. (*Pleasantly*) My name is Penelope. Mrs Violet Penelope.

TIM: (*Introducing himself*) Timothy Valentine – and this is Miss West.

MRS P: Oh, how do you do, my dear?

LINDA: How do you do?

MILLAIS: (*After a moment's pause – calling*) Steward!

STEWARD: Yes, Mr Millais?

MILLAIS:	Would you be good enough to get me a drink, please?
STEWARD:	Certainly, sir. What would you like, sir?
MILLAIS:	A ginger ale.
STEWARD:	Very good, sir.
TIM:	(*After a moment*) Are you going far, Mrs Penelope?
MRS P:	Well, I'm flying to Casablanca and then continuing my journey by train. (*Vaguely*) My destination is … Oran.

Music starts.

LINDA:	Oran?
MRS P:	Yes. Have you ever been to Oran, Miss West?
LINDA:	No, I'm afraid I haven't.
MRS P:	Oh, charming spot. Really delightful. So colourful – so quaint – so – so fascinating. (*A moment – almost a wistful afterthought*) Not far from Oran there is a place called Ras-el-Ma.

The plane engines rev up and open to full throttle.
CROSSFADE the plane engines to music.

CROSSFADE the music to the sound of the plane in steady flight.

MILLAIS:	(*Pleasantly*) Are you feeling any better now?
MRS P:	(*Breathlessly*) Yes, I'm feeling much better thank you. Much better. Oh dear, how very stupid of me to faint like that. How very, very, stupid!
LINDA:	Would you care to change places, Mrs Penelope? Perhaps if you sat by the window …

MRS P:	No. No, I think I shall be all right now, thank you.
TIM:	It's the altitude, I guess. If you're not used to flying it sometimes affects you that way.
MRS P:	But I am used to it, Mr Valentine! And it's certainly never affected me like this before. Oh dear! It must be old age creeping on!
MILLAIS:	(*Laughing*) Nonsense! Look! Let me tell the steward to get you a glass of soda water.
MRS P:	No! No, please – I shall be perfectly all right.
TIM:	(*After a moment, conversationally*) Are you flying to Casablanca, sir?
MILLAIS:	Yes, I'm flying to Casablanca and then later – I hope – on to Marapest. My card, sir. Philip Millais. Representing the European Branch of the Trans-Eurasian Oil Combine.
TIM:	Oh, thank you. Timothy Valentine – London Tribune.
MILLAIS:	(*Surprised*) Oh! I've read your articles many times, Mr Valentine.
TIM:	And this is …
MILLAIS:	(*Chuckling*) You've no need to tell me who this is! I've seen Miss West far too often not to recognise her. Delighted – delighted, Miss West. Are you staying in Casablanca?
LINDA:	Yes – for a little while – I hope.
MILLAIS:	At the Hotel Europe, of course.
LINDA:	Yes.
MILLAIS:	Good. You'll find it most interesting, I feel sure.
MRS P:	(*Weakly, controlling herself*) Mr – Mr Millais, do you think I might have that – glass of – soda water – after all?
MILLAIS:	(*Laughing*) But of course! Of course! (*Calling*) Steward! … Steward! …

CROSSFADE the last words down and the plane up.
CROSSFADE the plane to music with a vocal refrain.
At the end of the vocal refrain, FADE IN light chatter.
Music continues under the dialogue.

MRS P: (*Surprised*) Hello, Miss West – haven't you had dinner yet?

LINDA: (*Rather irritated*) No. I'm still waiting for Mr Valentine. He promised to meet me here on the terrace – at eight o'clock.

MRS P: Oh dear. Oh dear. How very annoying.

MILLAIS: (*Coming in – in a very good humour*) Hello, Miss West – hasn't the impertinent fellow turned up yet?

LINDA: No, I'm afraid he hasn't.

MILLAIS: Well, I told you not to wait! You should have had dinner with me when I asked you to. I know these newspaper men – no sense of time or responsibility. However – you don't deserve it young lady – but I've brought you a cocktail.

LINDA: (*Laughing*) Oh. Oh, that's awfully sweet of you.

MILLAIS: Are you feeling better, Mrs Penelope?

MRS P: Well, I'm still a little shaky, I'm afraid.

MILLAIS: You'll be more yourself tomorrow morning.

MRS P: Well, I hope so.

MILLAIS: I should have a good night's rest.

The music finishes about here.

MRS P: Yes. Goodnight, my dear – and a pleasant journey tomorrow.

LINDA: Thank you.

MRS P: Goodnight, Mr Millais.

MILLAIS: Goodnight. (*A moment, then*) What time was this Mr Valentine supposed to be meeting you?

LINDA: Well – he said eight o'clock.

MILLAIS: Eight o'clock! It's now a quarter to nine.

LINDA: Yes, I know.

(*Gently fade the background chatter*)

MILLAIS: I'm beginning to take a very poor view of that young fellow.

LINDA: (*A little laugh*)

MILLAIS: (*After a moment – pleasantly*) Aren't you going to drink your cocktail?

LINDA: (*Suddenly*) Oh! Oh, yes, of course.

DON QUISANDO arrives. He bumps into LINDA and the cocktail glass smashes to the ground.

LINDA: Oh!

MILLAIS: (*Intensely annoyed*) Why you clumsy fool, why don't you look where you are …

QUISANDO: (*Apparently horrified*) Senorita! A thousand pardons, Senorita! I did not realise that … Oh, Senorita, your dress! Your beautiful dress!

LINDA: (*Embarrassed*) It's all right! Really – it's quite all right!

QUISANDO: No! No! It is not all right! Senor! Senorita! I am most terribly sorry – I …

LINDA: It's quite all right – really – there's no harm done.

QUISANDO: But I was so clumsy! So stupid! I … Please! I beg of you! Please – accept my most humble apologies!

LINDA: Really, there's – nothing to worry about.

QUISANDO: But how could I be so stupid!

LINDA: Accidents will happen.

MILLAIS: (*Quietly*) Of course.

QUISANDO: You are most gracious, Senor. Most gracious. May I have the honour to present myself? Don Quisando. (*He clicks his heels*) At your service!

MILLAIS: Senorita West. I am Philip Millais.

31

QUISANDO:	Senorita – Senor Millais – once again – my most profuse apologies. Goodnight. (*He clicks his heels again*)
MILLAIS:	(*Calling after QUISANDO*) Goodnight.

A moment.

Suddenly LINDA and MILLAIS start to laugh.

LINDA:	What an extraordinary little man!
MILLAIS:	Did you notice his hair? And the moustache!
LINDA:	To say nothing of the perfume!

They continue to laugh.

WAITER:	(*Coming in*) Madam …
LINDA:	Yes?
WAITER:	Monsieur Valentine has arrived, madam. He is waiting for you in the restaurant.

Music starts.

LINDA:	And not before time! (*Laughing*) Goodnight, Mr Millais. Thanks for the cocktail!
MILLAIS:	(*Laughing*) Better luck next time!

FADE UP music, fading down the last words of MILLAIS' speech.

CROSSFADE music to a lift ascending.

The lift stops. Gates open and close.

TIM:	Well, here we are. This is your room, isn't it?
LINDA:	Yes.
TIM:	If you want me I'm on the next floor – 202.
LINDA:	Thanks. (*A moment*) I shall be all right.
TIM:	I'm awfully sorry about tonight – about keeping you waiting, I mean.
LINDA:	Oh, it couldn't be helped.
TIM:	I did intend to telephone but I thought perhaps you might change your mind and – well – have dinner with someone else.
LINDA:	Who for instance?

TIM:	Well, there's our Trans-Eurasion Oil friend – Mr Millais. He seemed particularly attentive on the plane, I thought.
LINDA:	(*Amused*) Well, as a matter of fact, he did ask me.
TIM:	There you are!
LINDA:	Would it have been so dreadful if I'd have accepted?
TIM:	Catastrophic!

LINDA laughs.

TIM:	What time are you leaving in the morning?
LINDA:	The boat sails at twelve.
TIM:	Oh. (*A moment*) Well, I hope you have a very pleasant trip.
LINDA:	Thank you.
TIM:	And you take care of yourself.
LINDA:	I'll try.
TIM:	(*Suddenly*) You know – you still haven't told me why you're going to Marapest.
LINDA:	(*Quite simply*) I did tell you. I'm going on a holiday.
TIM:	Oh, yes! Yes, of course. On a holiday.
LINDA:	Don't you believe me?
TIM:	(*A little laugh*) It sounds terribly phoney.
LINDA:	(*A shade defiantly*) Why shouldn't I go to Marapest for a holiday, if I want to? An awful lot of people do.
TIM:	An awful lot of people go to Blackpool. Where are you staying – The Martinique?
LINDA:	Yes. (*A moment – curious*) What's it like – exactly – Marapest?
TIM:	Haven't you seen the posters? Waving palm trees. Glorious silver beaches. Winding streets, thronged bazaars and glamorous

	women. You'll probably bump bang slap into Dorothy Lamour.
LINDA:	I don't believe it's a bit like that!
TIM:	Then you won't be disappointed.
LINDA:	No, seriously …
TIM:	It smells of dead fish and there's fifty million flies to every square inch.
LINDA:	Only fifty million?
TIM:	But each with a personal grievance.
LINDA:	It doesn't sound so hot.
TIM:	It's hot all right – but don't worry about that.
LINDA:	You've made me very happy. I can hardly wait to get there!
TIM:	(*Laughing*) Goodnight. If you want to get in touch with me you can always send me a cable care of the International Press Bureau, Casablanca – that'll find me.
LINDA:	Thanks. I'll remember that.
TIM:	Well – goodnight.
LINDA:	(*Faintly amused*) Goodnight.

Music starts to FADE IN.

TIM:	(*A moment*) Take care of yourself.
LINDA:	You said that before.
TIM:	Yes, well, don't forget. Keep your fingers crossed.
LINDA:	Goodnight.

As a door opens, FADE IN music, very distantly.
The door closes.

QUISANDO:	(*Quietly*) You've been a long time, Senorita.
LINDA:	(*A quick intake of breath*)
QUISANDO:	I've been waiting for you. (*Sharply, with authority*) Don't switch the light on – please! Please stand away from the switch!

34

FADE UP music a little.

LINDA: (*Tensely, bewildered*) Where are you? I can't see you! Where – are – you?

QUISANDO: (*Slowly*) I am in the armchair, Senorita – near the window – can't you see the cigarette?

LINDA: (*With a little start, as she notices QUISANDO*) Oh! What do you want? What – what are you doing here?

The music finishes.

QUISANDO: (*Suddenly, intensely amused*) What am I doing here, Senorita? What are you doing here – in Casablanca?

LINDA: (*Hesitantly*) I'm – on my way to Marapest.

QUISANDO: Ooh, Marapest. So – you are on your way to Marapest? The little Isle of muchio trama.

LINDA: Senor Quisando, I'm going to give you exactly two minutes. Tell me what you want and then – get out!

QUISANDO: In two minutes? You expect Don Quisando to tell you what he wants in two minutes? (*He chuckles*) You underrate my capacity for conversation. I have an insatiable appetite for the small details of life. (*Quietly, a sudden warning*) Your hand is near the switch, dear lady. Please. I do not wish to speak of that again.

LINDA: (*Tensely – frightened of QUISANDO*) What – do you – want?

QUISANDO: (*After a moment, curiously, and a little hurt*) Why is your voice trembling? Is it because you are afraid of me?

LINDA: (*Tremulously*) Senor Quisando, what is it you want?

35

QUISANDO:	From life, Senorita? A great deal. From you – if you please – a little patience. (*A moment*) Tonight, on the terrace, I introduced myself to you by the simple expedient of – knocking – a – cocktail – glass – out of your hand.
LINDA:	(*Surprised*) You did that deliberately?
QUISANDO:	Quite deliberately, and for the most excellent reason in the world. But let us suppose for a moment that I had <u>not</u> interfered. Let us suppose that you had <u>drunk</u> the cocktail that the gallant Senor Millais had so carefully prepared for you. (*A moment*) What do you think would have happened, dear lady?
LINDA:	Why – why, what possibly could have happened?
QUISANDO:	(*Quite simply*) I shall tell you. By this time tomorrow you would have been a very, very sick person. By the end of the week your friends would have been saying – "She was so charming, so gay, so full of life, it was a pity that – she – died – so – young."
LINDA:	(*Aghast*) Are you joking?
QUISANDO:	(*A moment, seriously*) I do not joke about such things.
LINDA:	(*Bewildered*) But – but look here, are you asking me to believe that this Mr Millais actually tried to – poison me?
QUISANDO:	(*Quite simply*) Don't you believe it?
LINDA:	Why it's preposterous! I hardly know the man! Besides, he seems a perfectly ordinary, respectable sort of person.

QUISANDO:	People are not always what they seem. Especially the most respectable ones. Why are you in Casablanca at this moment, for instance – instead of in London – at the theatre – where you belong?
LINDA:	I've told you I'm on my way to Marapest.
QUISANDO:	Yes, but why? (*A significant pause*) Because – you – hope – to – find – Roger Knight.
LINDA:	(*Quietly, tensely*) What do you know about Roger Knight?
QUISANDO:	I know that he is your brother and that he is supposed to have disappeared. Is that why you are going to Marapest?
LINDA:	(*After a moment*) Yes.
QUISANDO:	You are very beautiful, Senorita – and like most beautiful women very, very stupid. Please! Go back home. Take my advice. Do not interfere in things which you – do not understand.
LINDA:	(*Tensely*) Do you know my brother?
QUISANDO:	We have met.
LINDA:	When? When was the last time you met?
QUISANDO:	Oh – a little while ago.
LINDA:	Where?
QUISANDO:	(*A moment – reluctantly*) In Marapest.
LINDA:	(*Softly, to herself*) In Marapest …
QUISANDO:	Yes, but please, believe me! I know what I am talking about when I say to you – take care! Do not go to Marapest!

Music starts distantly.

QUISANDO:	I beg you to … (*He stops suddenly*)
LINDA:	(*After a moment*) What is it?

37

QUISANDO:	Nothing – nothing – but I must leave you now, Senorita!
LINDA:	(*Faintly amused*) I take it you have a very good friend in the orchestra, Senor!
QUISANDO:	What do you mean?
LINDA:	Doesn't that music mean that the police have arrived and that they are searching the grounds for her?
QUISANDO:	(*Quietly – surprised*) How did you know?
LINDA:	(*A little laugh*)
QUISANDO:	(*For a moment almost amused*) Perhaps you are not such a fool after all, Senorita.
LINDA:	Perhaps.
QUISANDO:	It is nothing. But in Casablanca the police, you know, they are so – so easily offended. Would you mind opening the window for me? I do not wish to be seen.

A pause and then the window is opened.
FADE UP the music a little.

QUISANDO:	If you are still stupid, dear lady – and insist on going to Marapest ... (*He hesitates*)
LINDA:	Yes?
QUISANDO:	Then let me give you – a – little – piece – of advice. (*Suddenly, no longer hesitant*) When you arrive on the island, make yourself known to a man called Smith. Tinker-Bell Smith. He has a little shop in the Rue de Tangier.
LINDA:	(*Quickly, tensely*) What sort of a shop?
QUISANDO:	(*Vaguely*) Ooooh – he sells dogs, cats, monkeys, all sorts of animals. He's a strange fellow this Tinker-Bell Smith but – who knows? – he might be useful to you. Tell him – Don Quisando sent you! (*A*

	chuckle) Goodnight, Senorita – and pleasant dreams!

FADE UP music, fading down the last words of speech.

CROSSFADE music to the lift descending.
The lift stops – the gates open – fade in busy chatter of the hotel foyer.
The lift gates close.

MRS P:	(*Coming in – pleasantly*) Hello, Miss West – just leaving?
LINDA:	No, I'm afraid I haven't finished packing yet.
MRS P:	What time do you sail?
LINDA:	Just after midday.
MRS P:	Well, I hope you have a very nice voyage – with the sea as calm as a mill pond.
LINDA:	(*Laughing*) Thank you. I hope so too. (*Suddenly*) Oh, Mrs Penelope …
MRS P:	Yes, my dear?
LINDA:	I've been meaning to ask you. When we first met – on the plane – you said something which rather intrigued me.
MRS P:	Indeed?
LINDA:	Yes, you said – (*Lightly*) "Not far from Oran there is a place called Ras-el-Ma".
MRS P:	Did I, my dear?
LINDA:	Yes. I – I wondered what you meant by that?
MRS P:	(*Seriously*) I meant you to know that you had a … (*Suddenly, a complete change of manner*) Ah, here's your friend, Mr Valentine! My word, he does seem in a hurry!

TIM: (*Coming in – rather curtly*) Oh, good! I'm glad you haven't gone. I want to have a chat. Come out on the terrace.

LINDA: But I haven't finished packing yet.

TIM: Good heavens, don't worry about that. I haven't even started.

MRS P: Oh dear! Are you departing us as well, Mr Valentine?

TIM: Yes, I'm afraid so. (*To LINDA*) I've got rather a surprise for you, Linda.

LINDA: What?

TIM: I'm going to Marapest.

LINDA: (*After a moment*) Oh.

TIM: You don't seem very pleased!

LINDA: I thought you were going to stay in Casablanca.

TIM: I was. I've changed my mind.

LINDA: Why?

TIM: (*Curtly*) Come out on the terrace and I'll tell you all about it.

MRS P: (*Moving away – laughing*) Goodbye, my dear! Goodbye, Mr Valentine!

TIM: (*Calling*) Goodbye!

Slowly FADE background chatter down and out.

LINDA: (*Irritatedly*) Well – what's all the mystery about?

TIM: (*Annoyed*) You're asking me? I like that, I must say!

LINDA: What do you mean?

TIM: You may be interested to know that, after I left you last night, I didn't go straight to my room.

LINDA: Oh?

TIM: I went down to the terrace.

LINDA: Well?

TIM: I was smoking a cigarette and thinking about nothing in particular, when suddenly an extremely excitable little gentleman made rather an undignified exit from a bedroom window.

LINDA: (*Softly*) Oh!

TIM: Now you must forgive the apparent curiosity, Miss West, but I find it a little difficult to understand why you should personally open a bedroom window in order to allow …

LINDA: (*Quietly, interrupting TIM*) His name was Don Quisando. I met him earlier in the evening on the terrace.

TIM: Indeed. (*A moment*) I take it he made quite an impression.

LINDA: (*Quietly, intensely angry*) Mr Valentine ….!

TIM: Then was it necessary for Senor Quisando to leave quite so hurriedly, and by the window?

LINDA: Senor Quisando invariably leaves by the window. Windows have a fatal fascination for him!

TIM: Indeed! (*After a moment – much calmer*) Don't you think it might be quite a good idea if we started putting our cards on the table? (*A tiny pause*) I know your reason for coming to Casablanca – for wanting to go to Marapest. I knew your reason the moment I saw you on the place. You're – looking – for – your brother – Roger Knight.

LINDA: Yes.

TIM: (*After a moment*) Let me tell you something, Miss West, something I only discovered myself this morning. At the beginning of this week a girl was fished out of the River Thames. She was dead – murdered. That girl, apparently, bore a strong resemblance to –

LINDA: To whom?

TIM: To you.

LINDA: What are you suggesting?

TIM: I am suggesting that someone blundered – that someone murdered – the – wrong – girl.

LINDA: (*Frightened*) Oh! (*Quickly and rather tensely carried away*) Listen! Last night, whilst I was waiting for you, Mr Millais bought me a cocktail. I was just going to drink it when suddenly the glass was knocked out of my hand by Don Quisando. Naturally, I thought it was an accident. So did Millais. But later – when I got to my room – Quisando was waiting for me.

TIM: (*Interested*) Yes?

LINDA: He told me that – the cocktail had been – poisoned.

TIM: Is that why Quisando went to your room – to tell you about the cocktail?

LINDA: Not entirely. He wanted to warn me. He wanted to warn me not to – go – to – Marapest.

TIM: (*A moment, then suddenly*) Why are you in such a hurry to go to Marapest? Your brother worked <u>here</u>, you know – quite a lot. For all you know he may still <u>be</u> here – in Casablanca.

LINDA: I don't think so. In any case, there's someone I want to see at Marapest. A man called – Peter Vandare.

TIM: (*Curious*) Peter Vandare?

LINDA: Yes. Do you know him?

TIM: No, but I've heard of him. He's a Canadian.

LINDA: Yes.

TIM: (*Quietly*) Why do you want to see this man Peter Vandare?

LINDA: Well, so far as I can gather, Vandare was the last person to see my brother before he disappeared. Roger gave him his wristlet watch with instructions to send it to London. When the watch was examined it was discovered that a message has been scrawled on the inside of the strap.

TIM: What was the message?

LINDA: It simply said "Not far from Oran there is a place called Ras-el-Ma".

TIM: (*Astonished*) But – how extraordinary! How perfectly extraordinary! That's what the woman said on the plane – the old dame – Mrs Penelope!

LINDA: (*Quietly*) Yes, I know. (*A moment, then suddenly*) Tim, do you know many people in Marapest?

TIM: Quite a few. Don't worry, I'll show you around all right.

LINDA: I wasn't thinking of that. I was wondering if you know someone called – Tinker-Bell Smith?

TIM: Tinker-Bell Smith? Good God, yes! (Laughing) Now he is a character, if you like.

LINDA: Don Quisando advised me to – contact him.

TIM: Why?

LINDA: He just said he might be useful to me.

TIM: O.K. Then we'll contact him. I'll soon take you to see Tinker-Bell Smith. I'll take you the first night we get there.

LINDA: Thanks.

TIM: (*After a moment*) I'm – I'm sorry I was rude just now.

LINDA: Oh, that's all right. I'm sorry too. (*A moment*) I suppose you're going to Marapest because you think there might be a pretty good story in all this?

TIM: That's roughly the idea.

LINDA: Well – I must finish packing. I'll see you on the boat.

TIM: (*Pleasantly*) There's no great hurry – stay and have a cocktail.

LINDA: (*With an uneasy little laugh*) No, I don't think I will – thanks very much.

43

TIM: No, of course. I suppose you're rather prejudiced against cocktails just at the moment?

LINDA: Yes. (*Laughing*) Yes …

They both laugh, but LINDA's laughter is the laughter of a person who is not too sure of either herself or events.
CROSSFADE laughter to music.

CROSSFADE music to a busy Eastern street effect – chatter of European and native voices – cars, animals, etc.
FADE UP into the foreground of an old, dilapidated Ford car – a honking motor horn at frequent intervals through the scene.

LINDA: (*Rather nervously*) Oughtn't we to be there by now?

TIM: (*Thoughtfully*) Yes … (*Raising his voice*) I say, Guiseppe!

GUISEPPE: (*A fat, sleepy, indolent fellow*) Monsieur?

TIM: (*Sternly*) Where is this place?

GUISEPPE: You ask me to take you to Tinker-Bell Smith's I take you to Tinker-Bell Smith.

TIM: Yes, but we've been driving for hours.

GUISEPPE: It's a long way. Take a lot of time. Cost a lot of money.

TIM: Yes, well, I'm only paying what's on the meter, so don't get excited!

GUISEPPE: (*Laughing*) Suit me! Suit me damn fine! The meter it say 200 makartos. It say 200 makatos for the last five year. Swell meter!

TIM: Yes, well, come on – take the lead out of your pants – we're in a hurry!

GUISEPPE: (*Grumbling, to himself*) You English, like Americanos, always in a hurry. Some day, you do so fast you catch up with yourselves.

44

The car continues then there's a screeching of brakes, the sound of a horn and angry voices from the road.

GUISEPPE: Get out, you damn fool son of a ...!

LINDA: (*Scared*) Oh! Do be careful!

GUISEPPE: (*Laughing*) I put the lead back in my pants – yes?

TIM: Don't talk so much – and keep your eyes on the road – or you'll knock somebody down.

GUISEPPE: (*Completely indifferent*) It no matter. Too many people anyway.

The car continues. The sound of the horn again, the screeching of brakes, and then the car pulls up and the engine ticks over.

LINDA: Is this the place?

TIM: (*Staring around*) Yes – yes, I think so.

The car door opens.

GUISEPPE: It's on the corner over there. The place with the shutters. It's all closed up. What you want to see Tinker-Bell Smith for anyway? You wanta buy a monkey, I sell you monkey.

TIM: We don't want to buy a monkey.

GUISEPPE: Does tricks.

TIM: (*Politely, acid*) We don't want to buy a monkey.

GUISEPPE: Plenty-good-tricks!

TIM: We don't want to buy a monkey!

GUISEPPE: Sometime he walk just like Charlie Chaplin. Sometime.

TIM: I don't care if he walks like Hedy Lamarr! We don't want to buy a monkey!

GUISEPPE: (*Unperturbed*) O.K. O.K. No hard feelings – you just don't want to buy a monkey. O.K.

TIM: Will you wait for us – and then take us back to the hotel?

45

GUISEPPE:	(*Without a moment's hesitation*) It cost you another twenty-five makartos – maybe more.
TIM:	Twenty!
GUISEPPE:	(*A moment's thought*) O.K. I wait.

Slowly FADE OUT the car ticking over during the next speeches.

LINDA:	(*Apprehensively*) I say, this does look a tumbledown sort of place.
TIM:	(*Laughing*) Well – what exactly did you expect?
LINDA:	I don't know, but I didn't expect anything quite like this.

TIM knocks on the door.

| TIM: | I think Guisepe's right – the place looks closed down to me. |
| LINDA: | Yes. |

TIM knocks again.

The distant sound of animals – monkeys, parrots, etc can be heard.

LINDA:	(*Quietly*) What was that?
TIM:	What?
LINDA:	Didn't you hear?
TIM:	(*Laughing*) It's probably from inside the shop. I warn you, you'll see all sorts of things. Cats – monkeys – tortoises …
LINDA:	It doesn't look to me as if we shall see anything – not even Mr Smith!
TIM:	(*Suddenly, quietly*) Hello – the door's unlatched. This place isn't closed after all!

The door opens to the clang of an old-fashioned spring shop bell. There's a bedlam of noise from the animals.

| LINDA: | (*Terrified*) Oh! Oh – I – I … |
| TIM: | (*Laughing*) It's all right – it's all right. Come on. |

The door closes. The bell tinkles again.

TIM: They're all in cages – they won't hurt you. Stand over here.

LINDA: (*After a moment – staggered*) What an extraordinary collection! What sort of a man is this Tinker-Bell Smith?

TIM: You'll soon see!

LINDA: (*After a longish pause – quietly, tensely*) He doesn't seem to be in.

TIM: Open the door again.

The door is opened and closes. The bell sounds twice. There's another outbreak of animal noises.

LINDA: Does he live here – on the premises?

TIM: I should think so. If he didn't, he wouldn't leave the door open.

LINDA: No.

TIM: (*Calling*) Smith! Anybody in? (*Pause*) Hello, there!!

More animal noises.

LINDA: He – he doesn't seem to be here …

TIM: No. Extraordinary! Perfectly extraordinary!

LINDA: (*Nervously*) Let's go shall we? I – I …

TIM: No. No, wait a minute. There's no hurry. Let's have a look round.

LINDA: (*After a pause*) What's this?

TIM: (*Casually*) What? Oh. Oh, it's a lizard.

LINDA: A liz … (*Suddenly, it dawning on her*) A lizard!!!

TIM: (*Laughing*) It's all right – it's stuffed!

LINDA: Oh – oh …

TIM: (*After a pause – quietly*) There's a curtain over there – looks to me as if there's a settee behind it. (*A sudden thought, laughing*) I bet a fiver the blighter's asleep on it.

LINDA: He couldn't sleep through this noise – surely?

47

TIM: You'd be surprised what the old rascal can do on
           half-a-pint of – the – local … (*He slowly stops
           speaking*)
LINDA: (*Tensely*) What is it?
TIM: (*Quietly, very serious*) Stay where you are. Stand
           still!
LINDA: (*Tensely, a whisper*) What is it?
TIM: Look – there's something showing – beneath the
           curtain – it's …

*A moment's pause – then sound of heavy curtains on rings
being flung back.*

LINDA: (*A moment's pause – then a loud, terrifying
           scream*).
TIM: My God, it's a woman! She's dead!
LINDA: (*Horrified, bewildered*) It's – it's Mrs Penelope!!

An outbreak of animal noises – utter bedlam.
Music starts.

END OF EPISODE TWO

EPISODE THREE

IN WHICH THERE IS
MUSIC IN THE AIR

ANNOUNCER: During a visit to the Isle of Marapest, Roger Knight, Foreign Correspondent of The Daily Graphic, has mysteriously disappeared. His sister – Linda West, the well-known actress – is invited by the British Authorities to fly to Marapest. When Linda takes her seat on the plane she discovers, to her astonishment, that Timothy Valentine, a recent acquaintance of hers, is to be a fellow passenger. She also makes the acquaintance of a Philip Millais and a Mrs Violet Penelope. Later, at Casablanca, Linda is warned against Philip Millais by a quaint flamboyant little man who introduces himself as Don Quisando.

Music starts.

ANNOUNCER: Don Quisando advises Linda to make the acquaintance of a man known as Tinker-Bell Smith who owns a pet shop in the Rue de Tangier, Marapest. On arrival at Marapest, Linda, accompanied by Tim Valentine, visits the pet shop owned by the mysterious Mr Smith.

FADE UP music.

CROSSFADE music to animal noises.

TIM: (*Calling*) Smith! Anybody in? (*Pause*) Hello, there!!

Animal noises.

LINDA: He – he doesn't seem to be here ...

TIM: No. Extraordinary! Perfectly extraordinary!

LINDA: (*Nervously*) Let's go shall we? I – I ...

TIM: No. No, wait a minute. There's no hurry. Let's have a look round.

LINDA: (*After a pause*) What's this?

TIM: (*Casually*) What? Oh. Oh, it's a lizard.

LINDA: A liz … (*Suddenly, it dawning on her*) A lizard!!!

TIM: (*Laughing*) It's all right – it's stuffed!

LINDA: Oh – oh …

TIM: (*After a pause – quietly*) There's a curtain over there – looks to me as if there's a settee behind it. (*A sudden thought, laughing*) I bet a fiver the blighter's asleep on it.

LINDA: He couldn't sleep through this noise – surely?

TIM: You'd be surprised what the old rascal can do on half-a-pint of – the – local … (*He slowly stops speaking*)

LINDA: (*Tensely*) What is it?

TIM: (*Quietly, very serious*) Stay where you are. Stand still!

LINDA: (*Tensely, a whisper*) What is it?

TIM: Look – there's something showing – beneath the curtain – it's …

A moment's pause – then sound of heavy curtains on rings being flung back.

LINDA: (*A moment's pause – then a loud, terrifying scream*).

TIM: My God, it's a woman! She's dead!

LINDA: (*Horrified, bewildered*) It's – it's Mrs Penelope!!

An outbreak of animal noises – there is utter bedlam.

LINDA suddenly starts to cry.

TIM: (*Tensely, with authority*) Linda – take a grip on yourself! Don't give way – now!

LINDA: (*Getting hysterical*) It's horrible! Horrible! Horrible!

TIM: Linda!

LINDA: (*Pulls herself together, then*) Is – is she really dead?

TIM: Yes.

LINDA: How? I mean, how was …?

TIM: (*Quietly*) She's been stabbed.

A tiny pause.

LINDA: (*Quietly – appalled*) Oh.

TIM: Wait a minute.

The sound of the curtain being drawn.

TIM: That's better.

LINDA: (*Bewildered*) Mrs Penelope … But <u>why</u>? I don't understand. I mean … Tim, what does it mean? What's the meaning of it all? We – we left her in Casablanca three days ago. (Slowly) Why should Mrs Penelope visit a …

TIM: (*Interrupting LINDA, urgently*) Listen! We're in a pretty tight spot! We've got to concentrate on getting out of it. Now the point is – what do we do? We can stay here and wait for Tinker-Bell Smith, or we can fetch the police, or we can go back to the hotel. If we go back to the hotel we've got time, at any rate, to do a certain amount of thinking – and just at the moment that seems to me to be pretty important. However, it's up to <u>you</u>. (*A moment*) What do you say?

LINDA: (*After a tiny pause*) Yes. Yes, we'll go back to the hotel.

TIM: (*Quickly*) O.K. Now you go back to the car and wait. If Guiseppe asks any questions just don't say anything. I'll be there in two or three minutes.

LINDA: (*Puzzled*) What are you going to do? (*Tensely*) Tim, what are you going to do?

TIM: (*Slowly, almost thinking aloud*) There's something damn queer going on and I'm going to try and get to the bottom of it.

LINDA: What do you mean?

53

TIM	I'm going to search Mrs Penelope.
LINDA:	Search …?
TIM :	(*Quickly, urgently*) Now don't wait, Linda – get back to the car.
LINDA:	Yes – all right.
TIM:	And, of course, not a word of this to Guiseppe.
LINDA:	Take care, Tim.
TIM:	Don't worry.

The sound of the curtain being drawn back again.
Music starts, fade up.

FADE DOWN the last note of the music.
FADE IN the sound of the Ford car ticking over at a standstill.
Footsteps coming in are heard.

GUISEPPE:	(*Calling*) O.K. You ready to go now?
TIM:	Yes, take us back to the hotel.

The car door opens and closes.

GUISEPPE:	I take you pretty nice way back. Very pretty. It cost you fifty-two makartos.
TIM:	Take us STRAIGHT back!
GUISEPPE:	(*Disgusted*) You don't wanna see the beach?
TIM:	No. Take us straight back!
GUISEPPE:	O.K.

The gear changes and the car starts away.

LINDA:	(*Quietly, very tensely*) Everything all right?
TIM:	Yes.

The sound of a klaxon horn.

GUISEPPE:	(*After a moment – conversationally*) You see Tinker-Bell Smith?
TIM:	(*Hesitantly*) Er – no, we – didn't see him.
GUISEPPE:	Oh. Too bad.

The klaxon sounds again.

GUISEPPE: (*Mischievously*) You like me to – take you – to see him – maybe?

TIM: What do you mean?

GUISEPPE: You say he's not in the shop. Right. Then he's at Enrico's.

TIM: Enrico's? What's that – a café?

GUISEPPE: Yes.

TIM: Where is it?

GUISEPPE: Oh, it's just around the … (*Correcting himself*) I take you. Cost forty-eight makartos.

TIM: What makes you so sure that's he's at Enrico's?

GUISEPPE: (*Impatiently*) If the shop is closed, if there is no Mr Smith – all right, all right – Enrico's.

The klaxon sounds again.

TIM: (*Quietly, seriously*) What do you think, Linda?

LINDA: (*Undecidedly*) I don't know.

TIM: (*Suddenly, making up his mind*) Yes, all right, Guiseppe – take us to Enrico's.

GUISEPPE: (*Pleased*) Alright, Senor. (*Quietly, delighted with himself*) Forty-eight makartos!

The klaxon sounds vigorously.

FADE OUT the car with the klaxon sounding.

FADE IN the sound of a piano being played rather indifferently and several voices raised in song with a background of a small, rather rowdy crowd. The song finishes. A concertina starts playing and the background chatter continues.

TIM: (*Quietly*) There's Smith – over at the bar.

LINDA: The big man playing the concertina?

TIM: Yes.

LINDA: Is he – drunk?

TIM: (*A little laugh*) No, no, he's always like that. Shall I fetch him over here?

LINDA: Yes. (*Suddenly, tensely*) Are you going to say anything about …?

TIM: Mrs Penelope?

LINDA: Yes.

TIM: (*Quietly*) No. No, I don't think so – not at first at any rate. We'll see what happens. I shan't be a minute.

The concertina slowly comes to the foreground and then peters out.

SMITH: (*A cockney voice – hoarse – rather petulant*) Hello! It's a long time since I seen you, mate!

TIM: (*Pleasantly*) I don't believe you remember me.

SMITH: (*Faintly aggressively*) Yes, I do. I don't forget faces.

TIM: (*A little laugh*) If you remember me I'll buy you a drink.

SMITH: (*Cocksure*) Timothy Valentine – Daily Graphic!

TIM: Well – Timothy Valentine, yes. But not The Graphic … The Tribune.

SMITH: Same pack 'o lies – so what the hell! Are you going to buy me the drink, china?

TIM: Sure. Come over to the table. I've got a friend over there – she'd like to meet you.

SMITH: (*Suspiciously*) What's she want to meet <u>me</u> for?

TIM: I really can't imagine.

SMITH: I don't like strange women. I don't like women at all if it comes to that.

TIM: (*Apparently indifferent*) O.K. – then we'll stay at the bar.

SMITH: Ha – flashy looking piece, anyway. What's she doin' in this God forsaken paradise?

A mechanical piano starts to play in the background.

TIM: Why don't you ask her? She won't eat you.

SMITH: Eat me! (*Suddenly, a great laugh*) D'you think I'm frightened of a skirt! Don't make me laugh, china.

TIM: Then come on!

Slowly FADE UP piano, then down again.

TIM: Well, here we are, Linda! Tinker-Bell Smith. Six foot two of pop and – poison ivy!

SMITH: How are you? Welcome to Marapest, lady – though God knows why you came here!

LINDA: Well, one of the reasons was to see you, Mr Smith.

SMITH: Oh. How's that?

LINDA: I'm hoping that you might be able to help me. I'm looking for a friend of mine called Roger Knight.

SMITH: Roger Knight? Never 'eard of 'im!

TIM: He's a newspaper man – on the London Graphic.

SMITH: What's he look like?

TIM: Oh, he's about medium height. Dark. Clean shaven. Round, pleasant sort of features – got rather a nice voice.

SMITH: No – never seen the gent. What makes you think I know 'im, anyway?

LINDA: (*Quietly*) Don Quisando told me that you might be able to help me.

The piano stops.

SMITH: (*Surprised*) Oh. (*Suddenly, rather petulantly*) Well, as a matter of fact I have met this friend of yours. Didn't recognise the description of 'im – but now I've got 'im all right! He came to the shop about six months ago.

TIM: What for?

SMITH: What the 'ell d'you think he came for? He wanted to buy something!

TIM: What?

SMITH: Well – I does a bit of buying an' selling on the side, you know. Not only pets an' things but antiques as well. This friend of yours had heard about a music-box I 'ad. Lovely thing. Made out o' walnut – continental walnut. He wanted to buy it.

TIM: Did he buy it?

SMITH: No, he didn't. (*Quickly*) Why? Are you interested in it?

LINDA: No, but …

SMITH: Well, in any case I've sold it. Sold it the very first day I 'ad it.

LINDA: (*Curious*) Who did you sell it to? Can you remember?

SMITH: O' course I can! I sold it to an American girl called Ruby Thompson – she works at The Villanova. That's a cabaret joint near the centre of …

TIM: (*Interrupting SMITH*) Yes, I know The Villanova. But tell me – did you tell Knight that you'd sold the musical-box to Miss Thompson?

SMITH: Yes, I think I did, but I'm … (*Suddenly*) Here, what is all this anyway? What's it all about? If you're not interested in the musical-box, then what <u>are</u> you interested in?

TIM: We've told you – we're interested in Roger Knight. (*Suddenly*) I'll get you a drink.

SMITH: No. No, I've changed my mind. I don't want a drink. I've got to get back to the shop – ought to have been there hours ago. If there's anything else you want to know, just pop in an' see me. If I'm not in the shop you'll find me here – at Enrico's.

TIM: O.K.

LINDA: And thanks.

SMITH: What for? You're welcome.

TIM: (*Suddenly, almost an afterthought*) Oh, by the way – do you happen to know a rather elderly lady called Mrs Penelope?

SMITH: Mrs Penel …?

TIM: Penelope. Mrs Violet Penelope.

SMITH: (*He obviously doesn't*) No. No, can't say I do … Why?

TIM: I wondered, that's all.

SMITH: Elderly ladies aren't much in my line. (*Going*) I'll be seeing you!

LINDA: (*After a moment – quietly*) He obviously doesn't know about Mrs Penelope.

TIM: No, I don't think he does.

LINDA: Did you find anything when – when you – searched …

TIM: No. There was a purse – but it was empty.

LINDA: (*Worried, nervously*) What are we going to do? Don't you think we really ought to go to the police?

TIM: No. We daren't take the risk. Not yet. Look here – you told me in Casablanca that you were going to Marapest to contact a man called Peter Vandare.

LINDA: Yes.

TIM: Who is Peter Vandare?

LINDA: I told you – he's the man who sent the watch through to London – to Major Hadley.

TIM: Yes, I know, but – who – is he?

LINDA: (*After a moment*) He's a member of the British Intelligence Service. Roger knew that – that's why he gave him the watch.

TIM: Then obviously Vandare is the person we ought to spill the beans to – about Mrs Penelope, I mean. We'll know exactly how to handle the affair and what we ought to do.

LINDA:	Yes, but I can't contact him! My instructions are to wait.
TIM:	How long for?
LINDA:	Well, they cabled Vandare that I should be arriving at Marapest on or about August the tenth.
TIM:	But that's five days ago.
LINDA:	I know.
TIM:	Well, I suppose we'll just have to sit tight and wait – that's all there is to it.
LINDA:	(*A moment – thoughtfully*) Tim – why do you think Roger went to see Smith in the first place?
TIM:	You heard what Smith said – your brother wanted to buy the musical-box.
LINDA:	Oh, but that's absurd.
TIM:	I'm not so sure. Anyhow, we can soon find out. I'll tell Guiseppe to pick us up tonight after dinner. We'll go down to The Villanova and have a word with that girl Ruby ...
LINDA:	Ruby Thompson.
TIM:	Yes. If your brother contacted her, then quite obviously he was after the musical-box.
LINDA:	But I fail to see why on earth Roger should ... (*She stops short*)
TIM:	What is it?
LINDA:	(*Quietly – astonished*) Look! Look who's here!
TIM:	Good lord! Millais! How extraordinary! How perfectly extraordinary!
MILLAIS:	(*Coming in – astonished*) Why, Miss West – this is a surprise! Ah – and Monsieur Valentine! How are you both? Never, in my wildest dreams did I expect to bump into you in a place like this! What on earth are you doing here?

TIM:	Oh, we're on a sort of Cook's tour! I'm showing Miss West the sights! (*With a laugh*) But what's more to the point, what the devil are you doing here?
MILLAIS:	You might well ask! I came in here to see who's car that is outside – the old Ford? I've been walking round this district for hours trying to find my way back to The Martinique! The people here! They are so dumb! So stupid! So …
LINDA:	Why? Do you – want a lift back to the hotel?
MILLAIS:	Do I want …? Oh, Miss West – those magic words!

They all laugh.

Music starts – FADING IN as laughter FADES OUT.

FADE DOWN music on the last note.

Knock on a door. The door opens.

| TIM: | Are you ready? |
| LINDA: | Yes, I've just got to put my hat on. |

The door closes.

TIM:	(*After a little pause – coming in*) M'm – and very nice too. Guiseppe's here.
LINDA:	Oh, good. (*Seriously*) Is that tonight's paper?
TIM:	Yes. There's nothing in it about Mrs Penelope. I've got a hunch the police haven't even found her yet.
LINDA:	But they must have found her. Smith said he was going back to the shop – so …
TIM:	(*Slowly*) Yes, but we don't quite know what he'd do – what his reactions would be. Even if he had nothing whatever to do with the actual murder he might get scared and …
LINDA:	And what?
TIM:	Dispose of the body.

61

LINDA: Yes. Yes, I never thought of that.

TIM: (*After a moment*) You haven't heard from Vandare, I suppose?

LINDA: No. Not a word. Have you seen Millais?

TIM: I noticed him while we were having dinner. He was over on the other side of the room.

LINDA: I thought I saw him. Tim – who <u>is</u> Philip Millais? And do you think he really tried to poison me that night on the terrace in Casablanca?

TIM: Yes, I think he probably did.

LINDA: (*Thoughtfully*) Then in that case, I wonder if I know the reason why ... (*Suddenly*) You see, after Roger had been in Marapest a little while he sent me a note, a note explaining that he'd discovered something – something pretty exciting – and that he intended to write me about it later. But he never did write to me.

TIM: Well?

LINDA: Well, I was just thinking. Supposing this man Millais imagines that Roger <u>did</u> write to me – so that now I know the secret – whatever it is – a secret that Millais doesn't want anyone *else* to possess.

TIM: (*Quickly*) That would explain the car crash and why he tried to poison you on the terrace in Casablanca!

LINDA: Yes.

TIM: (*Quietly, thoughtfully*) Yes – and to a certain extent it explains the behaviour of Don Quisando.

LINDA: Don Quisando? How?

TIM: Well – supposing this Don Quisando knows – or thinks he knows – that you possess the

	information, but he doesn't – possess – the information himself – yet.
LINDA:	Yes. Then that would explain why he saved my life, why he warned me against Millais, and why he tried to get into my good books generally.
TIM:	Yes.
LINDA:	Oh, if only someone would tell me what it was I was supposed to know!
TIM:	(*After a pause*) You know, I've got a hunch that the whole of this business centres round the musical-box.
LINDA:	Why do you say that?
TIM:	Well – your brother went to see Tinker-Bell Smith – obviously he had a reason. Mrs <u>Penelope</u> went to see Tinker-Bell Smith – so obviously <u>she</u> had a reason too. Philip Millais is here in Marapest – so it's pretty safe to assume that …
LINDA:	(Interrupting TIM) In other words, you think they're all here – or <u>were</u> here – for the same purpose – to find the musical-box?
TIM:	(*Thoughtfully*) Yes. Yes, I do. Don't you agree?
LINDA:	(*Puzzled*) I don't know. You see, if Roger was after the musical-box then why didn't he send Major Hadley a message about it instead of just a meaningless phrase like – 'Not far from Oran there is a place called Ras-el-Ma'? And secondly, don't forget, Smith was perfectly frank about the musical-box. He told us that he'd sold it to this girl Ruby – Ruby Thompson.
TIM:	Yes. (*A moment*) Well, we'll see what Ruby's got to say about things. Ready?
LINDA:	Yes, I'm ready.
TIM:	I've got Guiseppe waiting outside with that tin barouche of his.

63

FADE DOWN during the last words of speech.

FADE IN the old Ford car travelling with frequent use of the klaxon horn.

Background of Eastern street noises.

GUISEPPE: (*Talkative – in a good mood*) You have pretty swell plenty good time at The Villanova. Cost you a lot of money.

TIM: Keep your eyes on the road, Guiseppe – and don't talk so much.

The klaxon sounds.

LINDA: Where is this place?

TIM: It's just before you get to the docks – it shouldn't take us long.

LINDA: Have you been there before?

TIM: Oh yes – several times. It's run by a Greek called Nicky Dimitros.

GUISEPPE: I get you to the Villanova very quick tonight – leave it to Guiseppe.

The klaxon horn sounds again – the wheels skid as the car turns a corner.

FADE OUT street effects.

LINDA: It's very dark down here.

TIM: (*Quietly*) Yes, this isn't the main street. (*Raising his voice*) Guiseppe!

GUISEPPE: Senor?

TIM: Where the devil are you taking us?

GUISEPPE: To the Villanova!

TIM: Well – this isn't the main road.

GUISEPPE: You wanna go the main road? This is short cut – save a lot of money.

TIM: (*A moment – quietly*) O.K. Keep going. (*A pause – very quietly*) Listen – get well down in the car – snuggle down.

64

LINDA:	Why, what …?
TIM:	(*Softly, tensely*) Don't ask questions, just do as I tell you!
GUISEPPE:	(*After a moment*) You have plenty swell time tonight, I bet. Plenty dancing. Plenty drinking. Plenty good food. Swell place the Villanova. (*He starts to sing to himself – then changes to a gentle humming and finally stops*)

The car commences to slow down.

TIM:	(*Quietly*) What are you stopping for?
GUISEPPE:	There is an accident blocking the road, Senor. I shall have to stop the car and …
TIM:	(*Quietly, but with tremendous authority*) Listen, my fat friend – keep this chariot of yours on the move! Step on it!
LINDA:	(*Frightened*) What is it?
GUISEPPE:	Senor, I shall <u>have</u> to stop the car, I …
TIM:	(*Tensely*) Guiseppe, my sweet friend, stop this car and you're a dead duck!!
GUISEPPE:	(*Scared*) What do you mean?
TIM:	(*Steely*) Can't you feel it – on the back of your neck – nice – and cold?
GUISEPPE:	(*Terrified*) Senor!
TIM:	Now – keep going!

The car gathers speed again.

TIM:	Keep going! Step on it!! <u>Step on it!</u>

The car goes faster.

TIM:	Keep down, Linda!

The car crashes into a handcart and smashes it to smithereens – then goes on. Immediately following the crash there are angry shouts. Then two revolver shots and a sharp tinkle of glass is heard as a bullet shatters the windscreen. The car continues running.

TIM:	Is this the main road?

GUISEPPE:	(*A nervous wreck*) Si – si, senor.
TIM:	O.K. Now take us to The Villanova. And no short cuts! Savee?
GUISEPPE:	(*Weakly*) Yes, senor.
TIM:	(*Gently*) Are you o.k., Linda?
LINDA:	Yes. Yes, I'm all right.
TIM:	(*Faintly amused*) You can get up now.
LINDA:	Oh! Oh, thanks very much!
TIM:	Is this your hat?
LINDA:	Well, it <u>was</u> my hat!

TIM laughs.
CROSSFADE the laughter and the sound of the car to music.

CROSSFADE the music to the car running.
The car slows down, pulls up and ticks over.
The car door opens.

TIM:	Well, Guiseppe …
GUISEPPE:	(*Crestfallen*) What can I say, Senor? I am desolate! I am humiliated! I am …
TIM:	You can stop looking so sorry for yourself and tell us what happened.
GUISEPPE:	Well – tonight – while I wait for you at the hotel – a man came to me and – well – he offered me four hundred makartos if I would drive you down that alley tonight and stop the car. I do not like to do this, but – four hundred makartos is a lot of money, senor, and with …
TIM:	O.K. We'll skip it.
LINDA:	What was he like, this man?
TIM:	As if we didn't know! It was the fellow we picked up at Enrico's this afternoon, wasn't it, Guiseppe? The fat man – Monsieur Millais?

GUISEPPE: (*Surprised*) Why no, senor! No! This was a little man! A Spaniard. He called himself – Don Quisando …

LINDA: (*Aghast*) Don Quisando!

Music starts – full up – changes to a dance tune with RUBY THOMPSON singing "The Boys in the Back Room".

FADE IN boisterous chatter and laughter.

NICKY: (*Pleasantly, surprised*) Hello, Mr Valentine! How are you? I did not know that you were in Marapest!

TIM: Hello, Nicky! How's tricks?

NICKY: (*Laughing*) Oh, we get by, you know – we get by. Welcome to The Villanova, madam!

LINDA: Thank you.

NICKY: You would like a nice table near the stage?

TIM: No. Put us in a corner where we can talk.

NICKY: (*Chuckling*) Where you can – <u>talk</u>? This way, my friend!

LINDA: He obviously knows you of old!

TIM: Nicky's got a very nasty mind.

NICKY: But of <u>course</u> – it's good business! This way, madam.

FADE UP music and chatter for a few seconds, then FADE DOWN again.

NICKY: Now you want a nice bottle of champagne – oysters fresh from the bay – a little of our special Marapestachino, and then …

TIM: (*Quietly – interrupting NICKY*) Nicky, have you got a girl working here called Ruby Thompson?

NICKY: Sure! She ver' nice girl. But you got a girl, my friend!

TIM: What does she do exactly?

67

NICKY: Ruby? That's her singing now! Got some pretty swell pins! You'll like Ruby. Everybody likes Ruby. She's a great favourite.

TIM: I want to have a word with her, Nicky – send her over here.

NICKY: (*A moment*) Sure – sure – soon as she finishes this song.

TIM: Thanks.

NICKY: (*Going*) You're welcome!

FADE UP music to the finish of the number.
Loud applause and shouts of approval follow.

TIM: Our Miss Thompson can certainly do her stuff!

LINDA: (*Quietly, tensely*) Tim, do you think he was – telling the truth?

TIM: Who?

LINDA: Guiseppe?

TIM: Oh – you mean about – Don Quisando? I don't know. I'm damned if I do! After all, if Don Quisando had wanted to murder you, then why the devil didn't he do it in Casablanca? And there's another thing too, Linda – if Guiseppe was – (*He stops – softly*) Here comes our lady friend!

RUBY: (*After a moment – coming in*) Nicky tells me you wanted to see me?

TIM: Miss Thompson?

RUBY: Sure.

TIM: I'm Timothy Valentine of The London Tribune. This is a friend of mine – Linda West.

RUBY: Glad to know you.

LINDA: Won't you join us?

RUBY: Well, I've got another little number coming up right now, but …

TIM:	Well, join us when you've finished – we shall still be here!
RUBY:	(*Laughing*) O.K. I might do that. (*A moment – casually*) What exactly is it you want to – see me about?
TIM:	Well … (*He hesitates*)
LINDA:	Miss Thompson, do you know anyone called – Roger Knight?
RUBY:	Roger Knight? Why – why, sure, I … (*Hesitatingly, tense*) Is he a friend of yours?
LINDA:	(*Quietly*) He's my brother.
RUBY:	(*Taken aback*) Oh. Oh, I see.
TIM:	(*Slowly, curious*) About six months ago I believe you bought a musical-box from a man called Tinker-Bell Smith?
RUBY:	(*A moment, tensely*) Yes.
TIM:	Roger Knight came to see you about that musical-box – didn't he?
RUBY:	(*Hesitating*) Yes. Yes, I – believe he did.
TIM:	(*Quietly, but forcefully*) You know perfectly well he did! Now tell me, did the musical-box …?
RUBY:	(*Suddenly, completely flaring up*) Boy, am I sick to the back teeth of people talking to me about that musical-box! (*Completely exasperated*) I'm – just – sick – to – hell – of it! (*Desperately*) Listen! Listen, I've had just about enough of this! I'll blow the works wide open! I'll tell you the whole story right from A to ZEE! I NEVER BOUGHT A MUSICAL-BOX! What in hell's name would I want with a musical-box anyway? (*A moment*) You see honey, it started like this. One night Tinker-Bell Smith …

A roll of drums and cymbol crash is heard.

VOICES: (Shouting) Ruby! ... Ruby! ... Come along, Ruby!

Applause.

RUBY: Oh, heck! That's my number!

TIM: (*Quickly – tensely*) That's O.K. – the number can wait!

RUBY: No. No, I'll be back! Sit tight – don't go away. I'll come back to the table as soon as the number's over.

TIM: O.K.

LINDA: (*Quietly, very excitedly*) Tim – Tim, I really think we're going to learn something! I really think that at long last ...

Applause and shouts for RUBY build to a crescendo.

RUBY: (*Shouting*) Well, what is it tonight, boys?

VOICE: I'm in the Mood for Love!

Applause and shouts.

RUBY: O.K! O.K! If that's what you want – here it comes!

Applause and shouts.

The orchestra starts and RUBY sings I'm in the Mood for Love.

There is a storm of applause and shouts, gradually settling down to chatter and laughter after RUBY finishes.

LINDA: (*Tensely, anxiously*) Where is she? She's left the stage!

TIM: Yes. (*Suddenly*) Ah – ah, here she is!

RUBY: (*Coming in – breathlessly*) Well, I made it!

TIM: Would you like a glass of champagne?

RUBY: No. No, I never touch the stuff! But, gee – don't tell Nicky! (*A moment – slowly*) So you – want to hear about the music-box, eh?

LINDA: (*Anxiously*) Well, not only about the musical-box, Miss Thompson, but – about my brother.

Music starts.

RUBY: (*Quickly – rather sadly*) Yes. Yes, sure. He's a swell guy. He used to drop in here regularly, you know – almost every night. He first came to see me about ... (*Suddenly, almost desperately determined*) But look here, I said I was going to tell you the whole story, so – so help me! I'm going to tell you the whole story! One night – I guess it must be nearly six or seven months ago now – Tinker-Bell Smith suddenly took it into his head that ...

CROSSFADE the last words of speech down – music up to full to finish.

END OF EPISODE THREE

EPISODE FOUR

IN WHICH WE VISIT
THE EL BASSARI

ANNOUNCER:	During a visit to the Isle of Marapest, Roger Knight, Foreign Correspondent of The Daily Graphic, has surprisingly disappeared. His sister – Linda West, the well-known actress – is invited by the British authorities to fly to Marapest to try and find him. On arrival at the island, Linda – accompanied by a friend of hers, Timothy Valentine – visits a shop owned by a mysterious Mr Smith – Tinker-Bell Smith. Smith is not to be found at the shop however, but they discover, to their horror, the dead body of a fellow traveller – a Mrs Violet Penelope. Later the same day they meet Tinker-Bell Smith. He claims not to have heard of Mrs Penelope but states that Linda's brother – Roger – visited him several months ago in order to buy a musical-box, which he had already sold to an American cabaret singer named Ruby Thompson. Later the same night – and in order to make the acquaintance of Ruby – Tim and Linda visit the Villanova.

FADE UP music, bringing in the voice of RUBY THOMPSON singing I'm in the Mood for Love. The song continues to its finish.

There is a storm of applause and shouts, gradually settling down to chatter and laughter after RUBY finishes.

LINDA:	(*Tensely, anxiously*) Where is she? She's left the stage!
TIM:	Yes. (*Suddenly*) Ah – ah, here she is!

Gradually FADE DOWN noises to the background.

RUBY:	(*Coming in – breathlessly*) Well, I made it!

TIM:	Would you like a glass of champagne?
RUBY:	No. No, I never touch the stuff! But, gee – don't tell Nicky! (*A moment – slowly*) So you – want to hear about the music-box, eh?
LINDA:	(*Anxiously*) Well, not only about the musical-box, Miss Thompson, but – about my brother.
Music starts.	
RUBY:	(*Quickly – rather sadly*) Yes. Yes, sure. He's a swell guy. He used to drop in here regularly, you know – almost every night. He first came to see me about … (*Suddenly, almost desperately determined*) But look here, I said I was going to tell you the whole story, so – so help me! I'm going to tell you the whole story! One night – I guess it must be nearly six or seven months ago now – Tinker-Bell Smith suddenly took it into his head that he'd like to see me. He came down here and – well – over a drink or two he proposed what seemed to me a pretty crazy proposition.
TIM:	Go on.
RUBY:	Smith told me that he'd just bought a valuable musical-box. He said he didn't want to part with it but he wanted, if necessary, to give certain people the impression that he had sold it. And that, if I'd agree to say I'd bought it from him, he'd pay me two hundred dollars.
TIM:	Let's get this straight! Tinker-Bell Smith wanted to tell certain people, who might

	be interested in purchasing the musical-box, that you'd already bought it! And he wanted you, should it become necessary, to confirm this?
RUBY:	You've got it!
LINDA:	(*Puzzled*) And for that he was willing to pay you two hundred dollars? Why, that's ridiculous!
RUBY:	That's what I thought – but I went for it. I went for it in a big way!
TIM:	Well?
RUBY:	Well, he handed over the money and for the next two or three weeks nothing happened. Then one night – your brother turned up.
LINDA:	Roger?
RUBY:	Yes. He asked me about the musical-box and, according to plan, I told him I'd bought it from Tinker-Bell Smith. I hadn't got the thing, of course, so I said I'd sent it to a friend of mine in America. (*A little laugh*) Well – quite frankly – he didn't believe me. But he was quite pleasant about things and – well – he started to come here pretty regularly. (*Almost to herself*) He's a nice guy, that brother of yours ... Anyhow, to get on with the story. One night another man turned up – a fat, greasy sort of guy who called himself Philip Millais ...
LINDA:	Millais!
RUBY:	He asked me about the musical-box, too – and I dished out the usual story about buying it from Tinker-Bell Smith and

	sending it over to the States. He seemed to swallow it all right, and then he fairly took my breath away by saying that if I could get it back again he'd pay me twelve thousand dollars for it.
LINDA:	What!
TIM:	Twelve thousand dollars!
RUBY:	Yeah – twelve grand! You can imagine my feelings, brother! You could have knocked me down with a pair of fully fashioned! Twelve thousand dollars for a musical-box I'd never even seen! Well, that put me in a frap – one hell of a frap! I dashed round to Tinker-Bell Smith and I told him what had happened. "Tink" I said, "For Pete's sake let's have an eye-full of this musical-box! What's it play anyway – The Star Spangled Banner?" (*A moment*) And do you know what happened? He stood there in the middle of the floor – in the middle of that dirty, filthy little shop with the animals screeching their heads off and his trousers in tatters. He stood with his hair all over his head and a kind of cockeyed grin on his face, and he said – "Twelve thousand dollars, lady? What the hell do they think that is anyway? It's chicken feed! – Chicken feed – Chicken feed!" and the next thing I knew I was outside on the sidewalk.
LINDA:	But didn't – didn't you see the musical-box?
RUBY:	(*A little laugh*) Nope. I never caught so much as a glimpse of it! Anyhow, I made

78

my mind up – I made my mind up there and then. I decided to spill the beans. I went round to the Martinique. I knew your brother was staying there and I knew he was the only person I could possibly speak to. They told me he'd checked out. I left a message for him – I don't know whether he got the message or not, but – I've never seen him. I've never even heard from him. It's just as if he – completely – disappeared.

VOICE:	Ruby! C'mon, Ruby!
OTHER VOICES:	Yes. Come on, Ruby! Ruby! Ruby!

FADE UP background of shouts and laughter.

NICKY:	(*Coming in*) Come along, Ruby! Come along! We're all waiting for you! (*Pleasantly*) Everything all right, monsieur?
TIM:	Yes, everything's o.k.
NICKY:	That's swell! (*Going*) Come along, Ruby! The customers are waiting!
RUBY:	I must go … Goodbye.
LINDA:	(*Quietly*) Goodbye and thanks a lot!
RUBY:	You're welcome. If you see that hard hearted brother of yours you might tell him you bumped into Ruby Thompson.
LINDA:	We will.

A cymbal roll is followed by cheers, laughter and applause.

NICKY:	(*Coming in*) Ah! Here we are! Your oysters! Ab – so – lutely fresh, monsieur!
TIM:	Almost as fresh as the waiters, eh, Nicky?

They laugh.
RUBY and the ORCHESTRA perform Please Be Kind.
There is laughter and shouts during the song.

At the end of the song, applause, laughter and shouting is heard – gradually subsiding to background chatter and laughter.

TIM: She certainly knows how to put a number over, I'll say that for our friend Ruby.

LINDA: Tim, did you believe her story about the musical-box?

TIM: Yes. Yes, I believe it all right. (*Thoughtfully*) You know, Linda, I've got a hunch about all this business – I think I'm just beginning to see – exactly – how your brother fits into the picture. Roger knew something about that musical-box and he contacted Tinker-Bell Smith. Smith put him on to Ruby and Ruby dished out her usual story.

LINDA: But obviously Roger didn't believe her – she admitted that herself.

TIM: Yes. But shortly after contacting Ruby, Roger disappeared. Why? Well, if he didn't disappear of his own free will then obviously he must have been 'taken care of' for a particular reason. What was that reason? To my way of thinking it was one of two things. Either because your brother refused to swallow Tinker-Bell Smith's story about Ruby – or because he knew the real value – and the real secret – of the musical-box.

LINDA: (*Anxiously*) I only wish I could hear from Peter Vandare – after all, we do know that he was the last person to see Roger – and ...

Music starts again and continues under the dialogue.

TIM: And he might be able to throw some light on that extraordinary message? Yes ... You know, I've been thinking quite a lot about that

80

message. "Not far from Oran there is a place called Ras-el-Ma". It doesn't make sense to me, I mean, nothing we've heard or seen has had the slightest ... (*He stops*)

VANDARE: (*After a moment – coming in*) Pardon me – but is this seat taken?

TIM: (*Surprised*) Why – of course – the table's engaged. We ...

VANDARE: (*Seating himself*) Ah! What a relief! I don't know about you folks but this devil's temperature certainly gets me down. Phew! Now I ask you, how can a fellow feel a hundred per cent plus in this climate? (*Suddenly*) Oh. Oh, pardon me – I'm smoking – does that annoy you?

TIM: Not the smoking.

VANDARE: (*A moment – he chuckles*) That's very good. Very funny. Your friend has a sense of humour, Miss West. It – is – Miss West?

LINDA: Yes. I – have we met before somewhere?

VANDARE: No. No, unfortunately not. But we have, I believe, a mutual acquaintance. (*A moment*) Major Hadley ...

LINDA: (*Astonished*) Oh! Oh, you're – Peter Vandare?

VANDARE: Yes. Not quite what you expected, eh, Miss West? Come, tell me now, what did you expect? Someone younger – gayer – lighter? Not quite so ...?

LINDA: I don't know what I expected I'm sure, but – (*Almost with a sigh of relief*) I'm awfully glad to see you.

VANDARE: You have a friend, I see.

81

LINDA:	Yes, this is a very close friend of mine – Timothy Valentine.
TIM:	Of the London Tribune.
VANDARE:	Well – now, personally – I always read The Graphic – but …
TIM:	We can't all be well informed.
VANDARE:	(*Quietly*) Are you well informed, Mr Valentine?
TIM:	I know my way around.
VANDARE:	(*A chuckle*) If I may say so, my friend, that is not – quite – the same – thing. (*Suddenly*) Miss West, you are staying at The Martinique, I take it?
LINDA:	Yes.
VANDARE:	Perhaps we might have dinner together tomorrow evening – say, at eight o'clock?
LINDA:	Yes. Yes, I'd like to – very much.

The music finishes about here.

VANDARE:	Excellent! Excellent! (*Politely*) Are you enjoying your stay in Marapest?
LINDA:	(*Rather taken aback*) Well – I don't know whether I'm enjoying it or not. You see – I came here …
VANDARE:	(*Quickly*) Yes! Yes, we'll – er – talk about that tomorrow, Miss West.
LINDA:	Oh, you can talk quite freely in front of Mr Valentine. You see, he's …
TIM:	Quite well informed.
VANDARE:	I see. (*Suddenly, rather urgently*) I can't understand why you came here! I can't understand why Hadley sent you to Marapest!
LINDA:	But – but Roger was here! He was working here when he – disappeared …

VANDARE:	Didn't Hadley get the message? The message on the wristlet watch?
LINDA:	Yes – but …
VANDARE:	Surely that message indicated, more than anything else, that Oran should have been the real centre – the real centre for investigations. I feel quite convinced that your brother left for Oran shortly after he saw me.
TIM:	Did he definitely say that he was going to Oran?
VANDARE:	He told me that he hoped – in the very near future – to visit a place called Ras-el-Ma. (*Impatiently*) If I hadn't been up to my neck in routine stuff I'd have flown over to Oran weeks ago.
TIM:	(*Quietly*) Mr Vandare, I wonder if I might ask you a question?
VANDARE:	Surely.
TIM:	Supposing you went into a shop – a shop – somewhere in Marapest. Supposing you found someone in the shop – dead – murdered. Someone …
VANDARE:	Mrs Penelope?
TIM:	Yes.
VANDARE:	Don't worry about Mrs Penelope. That was unfortunate, but – these things happen.
Music starts.	
TIM:	Then you know?
VANDARE:	Yeah.
LINDA:	Who <u>was</u> Mrs Penelope?
VANDARE:	(*A moment – slowly*) Her name was Reece. She was a British agent. She went to the shop shortly before you did, Millais followed her and … well, I'll – I'll tell you all about Mrs

83

	Penelope tomorrow ... (*Suddenly*) Perhaps we shall meet again Mr Valentine – I'd kinda like that.
TIM:	Thank you – I'd like that too.
VANDARE:	Excellent! Excellent! (*He rises heavily – reluctantly*) Ah, well ... Goodnight, Miss West. Eight o'clock at The Martinique.

FADE UP music to full, FADING OUT the background chatter.

FADE music right down, fading in chatter and laughter in the background.

NICKY:	(*Coming in*) You are leaving us, monsieur?
TIM:	Yes. Goodnight, Nicky!
NICKY:	I hope you enjoyed yourself, madam.
LINDA:	Yes, thank you, I ... (*She stops*)
TIM:	(*Quietly, surprised*) Hello, Smith!
SMITH:	(*Coming in*) Evening all!
NICKY:	(*Annoyed and perturbed*) What do you want, Tinker-Bell? I've told you not to come to The Villanova! Go away! You cause a lot of trouble! Always you cause a lot of trouble!
SMITH:	Keep your hair on, mate! I'm not going to bust up the joint! (*To TIM*) Are you just leaving?
TIM:	Yes.
SMITH:	Lucky I caught you. (*Abruptly*) Nicky! 'Op it!
NICKY:	Now listen to me ...
SMITH:	You heard what I said, Nicky, 'Op it! Scram! Vamoose!
TIM:	(*Quietly*) That's all right, Nicky.
NICKY:	(*Warningly, going*) If I catch you touching anything, Tinker-Bell, I'll ...

SMITH laughs.

TIM:	Well, what is it?
LINDA:	What is it you want, Mr Smith?
SMITH:	(*Quite civilly*) Why didn't you tell me the truth? Why – didn't you tell me that he was your brother?
LINDA:	(*Softly*) How did you find out?
SMITH:	I found out all right – I find out most things round here when it comes to a push!
TIM:	You didn't come all this way just to tell Miss West that you know who she was.
SMITH:	No, I didn't. You're quite right, china. I didn't.
TIM:	Well?
SMITH:	(*A moment, then suddenly*) How would you like to see that brother of yours – tonight?
LINDA:	(*Staggered*) Are – are you serious?
SMITH:	(*Softly – urgently*) Listen! There's a little café called The El Bassari. It's in the native quarter about half a mile from here. You take the first turn to the right over the river and keep straight on – it's in the Rue Galicia. When you get there tell the waiter you wish to see Monsieur Andrianopolis.

Music starts and continues to play under the dialogue.

TIM:	(*Quietly, but forcefully*) Tinker, listen! If this is a trap – if this is a trap then, by God, I'll …
SMITH:	(*Interrupting TIM*) If this is a trap there's nothing you can do about it, mate – an' you know it! You've got to take a chance. It's up to you.
TIM:	Café El Bassari – Rue Calicia – ask for Monsieur Andrianopolis.
SMITH:	Yes.
TIM:	(*Suddenly, having made up his mind*) O.K., Tinker. O.K.

FADE UP music to full, fading out background effects.

FADE music slowly down and out.

FADE IN footsteps – TIM and LINDA – walking. In the background are faint river noises.

LINDA: We turn right here, don't we?

TIM: Yes – yes, I think we do.

LINDA: It's so terribly dark.

TIM: He said first right over the river – Rue Galicia.

LINDA: Yes. (*Anxiously*) Tim, do you think we really shall see Roger – or …

TIM: I don't know. But I've been thinking, Linda – it might be quite a good idea if I took you back to the hotel and then investigated this business myself.

LINDA: Oh, no, Tim! Please! Please, I … (*She stops, quietly*) What is it?

The footsteps stop.

TIM: Listen!

LINDA: (*After a moment – tensely*) What is it?

TIM: Didn't you hear anything?

LINDA: No. No, I don't think so. Only the river.

TIM: I thought I heard – footsteps. I … Perhaps I'm wrong.

The footsteps start again.

LINDA: I've got to come with you, Tim. I'd never stand it just waiting – just waiting to see if … (*She stops talking again. A moment, quietly*) I think you're …

TIM: (*Quietly*) Keep walking …

LINDA: (*Tensely*) What is it?

TIM: There's someone following us … I thought I heard him when we crossed over the river …

LINDA: (*Tensely*) What are we going to do?

TIM: Wait till we get to the corner. When we turn it, stand flat against the wall – and whatever you do, Linda, keep behind me.

LINDA: All right.

TIM: There's no need to be scared. Just keep calm.

LINDA: Yes. Yes, all right.

A pause.

The footsteps continue.

TIM: Here we are. Now, when we get round the corner – stand flat against the wall.

The footsteps continue for a moment – then stop.

A pause – then distant footsteps are heard.

LINDA: You can hear him now all right.

TIM: Yes. What's the betting it's our old friend Millais?

LINDA: Here he is.

TIM: Sh!

The footsteps approach into the foreground and stop suddenly.

MILLAIS: (*A gasp of surprise – then:*) What – what's the meaning of this ... Why ...

TIM: (*Sharply*) Drop that revolver ... Drop it, Millais, or ...

The clatter of the revolver on the pavement.

TIM: Pick it up, Linda.

MILLAIS: Why – why, Mr Valentine – what on earth ...?

TIM: Listen, Millais – you've been following us! You've followed us ever since we left The Villanova. Now what's the game? What's the sweet little game, my friend?

MILLAIS: (*Breathlessly*) I really don't know what you're talking about. I – I ... (*Suddenly a note of desperation*) Listen! It's no good beating about the bush any longer! It's time we put our cards on the table.

TIM: I couldn't agree with you more, my friend! Now suppose you start talking.

MILLAIS: (*Irritated*) We can't talk here. Why ...
TIM: (*Threatening MILLAIS*) Start talking!
LINDA: (*After a moment – quietly*) In London, Mr Millais, you tampered with my car so that there'd be an accident. In Casablanca, you tried to poison me. And then tonight –
TIM: Tonight, my friend – on the way to The Villanova – you arranged a nice little short cut for us – on top of which I feel quite sure you bribed Guiseppe to pass the buck on to a gentleman known as Don Quisando. Now, I suggest, Mr Millais ...
MILLAIS: (*Angrily*) We can't talk here.
TIM: Talk!
MILLAIS: (*Crisply, more certain of himself*) I don't deny what you say. It's true – all of it – but – well – I've been a little stupid, perhaps – a little over hasty. Now listen, my friends! It's time we got together over this business. There's plenty in it for all of us. Where's the musical-box? Has Smith got it, or did he really sell it to that damned cabaret artist?
TIM: (*Quietly*) Supposing, first of all, you tell us why – you want – the musical-box.

The distant sound of a car approaching is heard.

MILLAIS: What do you mean? Are you joking? You know perfectly well why I want it – you know perfectly well why we all want it.
TIM: Nevertheless, suppose you ...
LINDA: (*Quickly*) Tim, there's a car coming!
TIM: You heard what I said, Millais, why – do you want – the musical-box?
MILLAIS: (*Bewildered*) Are you serious? Do you really mean to tell me that you know nothing about ...

88

FADE UP the car into the foreground. A sudden burst of revolver shots is heard, then the car recedes into the distance. LINDA screams.

MILLAIS gives out a gasp of pain.

TIM: My God! Linda, are you all right?

LINDA: (*Faintly*) Yes. Yes, I … (*Horrified*) Oh! Look at Millais! Tim, look at Millais!

MILLAIS: (*Weakly, gasping*) I recognised him – I recognised him. It was … it was …

TIM: (*Quietly, after a moment*) He's dead.

VOICES: (*Distantly*) What was it? … I heard shots … It was this way … Somebody screamed … (*Etc*)

TIM: (*Quickly*) Linda, give me your hand! (*Desperately*) Quickly – give me your hand! Now – run! Run like the devil!

Running footsteps.

LINDA: (*Panting*) Tim – I …

TIM: Round here – come on!

The running footsteps continue.

LINDA: (*Trying to talk – breathlessly*) I – I don't – don't – know – why …

TIM: (*Equally breathless*) Wait – wait a minute!

The footsteps slow down and stop.

Slight pause.

TIM and LINDA gradually regain their breath.

LINDA: Did – did anyone see us?

TIM: No. No, I don't think so.

LINDA: Tim – Tim, who was it in the car?

TIM: I don't know. I didn't see him – I didn't even see the number plate.

LINDA: Millais saw him.

TIM: Yes, and he obviously recognised him. My God, this is a pretty kettle of fish and no mistake! Still, I appear to have been right about one thing. This business turns on the musical-box all right – and how!

LINDA: Tim, I don't understand it! I – I really don't understand it.

TIM: Don't worry about that, Linda. I don't understand it myself if it comes to that. And yet – I don't know, but – things seem to be working out all right. I always figured that Philip Millais was playing a lone game and now I'm pretty certain he was.

LINDA: You don't think that Don Quisando, Tinker-Bell Smith and Roger are all after the musical-box? You don't think that one of those three murdered Millais?

TIM: Tinker-Bell Smith might have murdered Millais, or even Don Quisando – but your brother certainly didn't, that's too silly for words. (*A moment*) I wonder if Smith was telling the truth about your brother.

LINDA: About him being at this – café place?

TIM: Yes. (*Thoughtfully*) Café El Bassari – Rue Galicia. Well, here we are – this is the Rue Galicia.

LINDA: There's a light showing on the corner – it looks as if it might be a night club or something.

TIM: Yes. Come on. Come on, we'll try it!

Footsteps as they walk along the street.

They slow down and stop.

LINDA: This looks a dreadful sort of place.

TIM: Yes, but – this is it all right. Look – over the door – Café El Bassari. Y.K. Andrianopolis.

Music starts – not faded up.

LINDA: Yes.

TIM: Come on. And whatever you do, Linda – stick close to me.

Two or three footsteps. The door opens – FADE UP music and laughter and chatter.

CARLOS: (*An old Frenchman, rather flustered*) I'm sorry, monsieur – we are full tonight – absolutely full – so if …

TIM: (*Quietly, but with authority*) Are you Monsieur Andrianopolis?

CARLOS: (*Calmer*) No, monsieur.

TIM: I'd like to see him, please. My name is Valentine.

CARLOS: You – have – an appointment?

LINDA: He's expecting us.

CARLOS: Monsieur Valentine?

TIM: Yes – Timothy Valentine.

CARLOS: (*A moment, on his guard*) You are from Tinker-Bell Smith, perhaps?

TIM: Yes.

CARLOS: Wait here, please.

Music finishes about here. There is a smattering of applause then the music starts again.

LINDA: (*After a moment - nervously*) Tim – Tim, do you really think that we shall see Roger?

TIM: (*Puzzled*) I don't know. By George, this business is extraordinary! Perfectly extraordinary.

LINDA: What I can't understand is why Vandare didn't tell us about Monsieur Andrianopolis! Surely if Roger is here then …

TIM: (*Quietly*) Then you'd think that Vandare would know all about it?

LINDA: Yes.

TIM: Unless of course … (*He hesitates*)

LINDA:	Unless what?
TIM:	(*After a moment*) Unless of course Tinker-Bell Smith was lying!
LINDA:	In which case …
TIM:	In which case we've certainly walked into a pretty nice trap.
LINDA:	(*Quickly, softly*) Here's the waiter!
CARLOS:	(*Coming in*) This way, please, madam – s'il vous plait, monsieur.

Footsteps.

FADE music slowly up, then slowly down a little.

A door opens – two or three footsteps, FADE music and chatter down slightly. The door closes, FADE music right down and chatter out. Six footsteps. Door opens.

CARLOS:	Monsieur Andrianopolis is waiting for you.
TIM:	Come on, Linda.

Door closes.

FADE out music.

QUISANDO:	Welcome to the El Bassari, Senorita West.
LINDA:	(*Staggered*) Why – why, Don Quisando!
TIM:	What!

Music starts.

QUISANDO starts to chuckle.

CROSSFADE the laughter out and music up to full.

FADE down music on the last note, fading in dialogue.

QUISANDO:	(*Still chuckling*) So Tinker-Bell Smith sent you to the Café El Bassari?
LINDA:	He told us that my brother was here – and …
TIM:	And if he's not here, my Spanish friend, we'd like a pretty snappy explanation – tout-de-suite, savee?
QUISANDO:	Your French is perfect, senor – how could one fail to understand you? However – you did not come to the El Bassari to talk with Don

	Quisando. You came to see Roger Knight. (*Moving away*) So – if you would be so kind – step this way.
TIM:	(*Suddenly*) Quisando!
QUISANDO:	(*A little away*) Senor?
TIM:	You will observe, I trust, that my right hand is in the pocket of ...
QUISANDO:	Your right hand is resting on a revolver, senor – on the trigger of a revolver. If there is any – er – funny business you will press that trigger. Correct, senor?
TIM:	Your English is perfect, Don Quisando. How could one fail to understand you?
QUISANDO:	(*Chuckles, then:*) This way, senorita ... senor.

A door slides open.

LINDA:	(*Puzzled*) What is this – a box-room?
QUISANDO:	No! No! It's an elevator – lift, senorita! I am taking you up to the third floor.
TIM:	Can't we walk?
QUISANDO:	There are no stairs.
TIM:	O.K. After you, senor.
QUISANDO:	(*Chuckling*) Gracias, senor.
TIM:	(*Quietly*) O.K., Linda.

Pause.

The sliding door closes.

QUISANDO:	(*Delighted with the turn of events*) Well, this is the moment you have been waiting for, senorita. Roger will be so pleased to see you. I feel – I feel so happy for you both! (*Suddenly*) Would you mind pressing the button, senor? Near your elbow – the third floor.

A moment's pause, then the lift starts to ascend.

Music starts.

CROSSFADE the lift out and the music up to full to finish.

END OF EPISODE FOUR

EPISODE FIVE

IN WHICH THERE ARE
CARDS ON THE TABLE

ANNOUNCER:	During a visit to the Isle of Marapest, Roger Knight, Foreign Correspondent of The Daily Graphic has mysteriously disappeared. His sister – Linda West, the well-known actress – is invited by the British authorities to fly to Marapest to try and find him. On arrival at the island, Linda – accompanied by a friend, Tim Valentine – visits a shop owned by a mysterious Mr Smith – Tinker-Bell Smith. Later the same night, Smith advises them to visit the Café El Bassari and make the acquaintance of a Monsieur Andrianopolis.

Music starts.

ANNOUNCER:	On arrival at the café, Linda is surprised to discover that Monsieur Andrianopolis is an old – and somewhat mysterious acquaintance of hers – known as Don Quisando.

FADE UP music to full – then down and out under the dialogue.

QUISANDO:	(*Chuckling*) So Tinker-Bell Smith sent you to the Café El Bassari?
LINDA:	He told us that my brother was here – and …
TIM:	And if he's not here, my Spanish friend, we'd like a pretty snappy explanation – tout-de-suite, savee?
QUISANDO:	Your French is perfect, senor – how could one fail to understand you? However – you did not come to the El Bassari to talk with Don Quisando. You came to see

97

	Roger Knight. (*Moving away*) So – if you would be so kind – step this way.
TIM:	(*Suddenly*) Quisando!
QUISANDO:	(*A little away*) Senor?
TIM:	You will observe, I trust, that my right hand is in the pocket of ...
QUISANDO:	Your right hand is resting on a revolver, senor – on the trigger of a revolver. If there is any – er – funny business you will press that trigger. Correct, senor?
TIM:	Your English is perfect, Don Quisando. How could one fail to understand you?
QUISANDO:	(*Chuckles, then:*) This way, senorita ... senor.

A door slides open.

LINDA:	(*Puzzled*) What is this – a box-room?
QUISANDO:	No! No! It's an elevator – lift, senorita! I am taking you up to the third floor.
TIM:	Can't we walk?
QUISANDO:	There are no stairs.
TIM:	O.K. After you, senor.
QUISANDO:	(*Chuckling*) Gracias, senor.
TIM:	(*Quietly*) O.K., Linda.

Pause.

The sliding door closes.

QUISANDO:	(*Delighted with the turn of events*) Well, this is the moment you have been waiting for, senorita. Roger will be so pleased to see you. I feel – I feel so happy for you both! (*Suddenly*) Would you mind pressing the button, senor? Near your elbow – the third floor.

A moment's pause, then the lift starts to ascend.

QUISANDO:	Ah! Gracias, senor – gracias!

The lift continues for a few seconds, then stops. The sliding door opens.

LINDA: (*With a cry of delight*) Roger! Darling – you – really are here!

ROGER: (*Delighted at seeing LINDA*) Hello, Linda! Gosh, I'm glad to see you! Hello, Tim – how are you?

The sliding door closes in the background.

TIM: (*Obviously surprised*) I'm fine – but you've certainly been leading us a dance, old boy!

ROGER: (*Laughing*) Yes, I know but …

QUISANDO: Let's go to your room, senor – we can't talk here …

A door opens.

LINDA: Roger, are you all right, darling?

ROGER: (*Brightly*) Yes. Yes, I'm all right.

LINDA: You've lost an awful lot of weight.

ROGER: I'm fine, Linda. I've been having a pretty rough trip but I'm fine. Gosh, I'm glad to see you again!

QUISANDO: You've been having a rough trip, senor! And what about Don Quisando? And with Monsieur Millais come to that.

LINDA: (*Suddenly, anxiously*) Roger, darling – tell me … (*She stops*)

ROGER: Tell you what, Linda?

LINDA: Did you … (*She hesitates*)

TIM: (*Quietly*) Your sister is trying to ask you whether you – murdered – Philip Millais?

ROGER: (*Staggered*) Murdered Philip Millais?

QUISANDO: (*Quickly, tensely*) Is Millais dead?

TIM: Yes.

ROGER: (*Staggered*) What!

QUISANDO: Are you certain, senor – absolutely certain?

TIM: Of course I'm certain.

LINDA: We were there when it happened, Roger – both of us. You see, Millais had followed us from The Villanova – and …

TIM: (*Interrupting LINDA*) Just a minute, Linda. Now look here, Roger – for the past week or so your sister and I have had a pretty hectic time. A great many things have happened which we neither understood nor, quite frankly, liked the look of. I think you owe us an explanation.

LINDA: Why did you disappear so suddenly, Roger? What happened? Are you hiding from something – or someone?

ROGER: (*Quietly, rather intrigued*) Tim – tell me – how did you get mixed up in this business?

TIM: Well – your sister had a car accident in London and I happened to be on the spot when it happened. Later, when I boarded a plane for Casablanca, she was on board en route for Marapest. I guessed why. I knew that she was coming out here to …

QUISANDO: To look for Roger.

TIM: Yes. When I arrived at Casablanca I received a cable. A girl had been brutally murdered – a girl who bore a strong resemblance to Linda West. I suddenly remembered the car accident and – well – put two and two together.

QUISANDO: You guessed that someone had murdered the wrong person?

TIM: Yes.

LINDA: But why should anyone wish to murder me – of all people?

ROGER:	(*Quietly*) I'm grateful to you, Tim, for looking after Linda, but – but I wish …
LINDA:	He's been wonderful, Roger – almost like a brother.
TIM:	That wasn't entirely my intention, however – you were going to say?
ROGER:	I was going to say – I wish you hadn't come here, Linda. You see … (*He hesitates*)
QUISANDO:	It would be wiser, senor, to start your story from the beginning.
ROGER:	Yes. (*A moment*) Tim, you've heard of Kurt Van Zyland?
TIM:	(*Staggered*) Kurt Van Zyland? Good lord yes! Why before the war Scotland Yard and the F.B.I. would have given a fortune to have laid hands on Kurt Van Zyland. If you could have nabbed Van Zyland, old boy, you'd have turned yourself into an international figure overnight!
LINDA:	I remember reading about Van Zyland. He was killed.
TIM:	He was killed in an air raid shortly after …
ROGER:	(*Suddenly*) Kurt Van Zyland is alive! He's not only alive, but he's here – here in Marapest!
TIM:	What!
ROGER:	Now listen! Just before 'D' Day, about three and a half million pounds worth of jewels were taken from France by a man called Otto Kyfhausser. Those jewels were concealed by Kyfhausser somewhere in the Bavarian Alps. Kyfhausser made a plan – a plan of the exact whereabouts of the stolen jewels.
TIM:	Go on.

ROGER:	He divided the plan into two parts. The first half of the plan he kept himself – and the second half he handed over to Kurt Van Zyland. It was agreed that if anything should happen to Kyfhausser, <u>his</u> half of the plan should be delivered to Van Zyland.
TIM:	Well?
ROGER:	Well – something did happen to Kyfhausser. He was involved in an aeroplane crash and received fatal injuries. But – the first half of the plan never reached Van Zyland.
LINDA:	How do you know?
ROGER:	Because Kyfhausser handed it to me – just before he died!
TIM:	Handed it to <u>you</u>?
ROGER:	Yes. Kyfhausser died in a field hospital on the outskirts of Duisberg. He was in a pretty bad way and I had a devil of a job understanding half of what he said. But he confessed about the loot and asked me to deliver his part of the plan, carefully concealed in a musical-box, to Van Zyland at an address here in Marapest.
LINDA:	In a musical-box!
ROGER:	Yes. Well, actually my first thought was to report the whole thing to British Intelligence and come back to England. Then, suddenly, I had an idea.
QUISANDO:	The craziest, stupidest, maddest idea you've ever heard of, senor!
ROGER:	(*Quietly*) I made up my mind to capture Kurt Van Zyland.
LINDA:	(*Doubtfully, almost reproaching ROGER*) Oh, Roger!

TIM:	My dear Roger, for the past fifteen years the police force of the entire Continent have …
ROGER:	But don't you see, Tim! Don't you see! I'd got something Van Zyland wanted! I'd got something Van Zyland wanted more than anything else in the world. The musical-box.
LINDA:	But didn't this man Kyfhausser tell you where the jewels …
ROGER:	Where the loot was hidden? No, he was in a pretty bad way and it was just about all the poor devil could do to tell me about the musical-box. Anyway – I came to Marapest. But Van Zyland must have known something had gone wrong because by the time I'd got here, he'd carefully disappeared. So I contacted Tinker-Bell Smith. He was an old friend of mine and he did exactly what I wanted him to do, he started to talk – he let it be known that he'd just bought a valuable musical-box and that, providing the right customer came along, he was willing to sell it. Years ago, Smith had met Van Zyland – and I knew that once he showed up, Tinker-Bell would recognise him all right. Well – Tinker-Bell spread that story around for all it was worth – but Van Zyland was taking no chances – he still laid low.
QUISANDO:	You see, senor – Van Zyland still possesses half of the plan – he's therefore in what you might call a pretty strong position. Also, he knows only too well that nothing can be done about the jewels until things in Europe have become – well – considerably more stabilised, so he is in no hurry.

TIM: Yes. Yes, I can see that all right. But how exactly do <u>you</u> fit into the picture, Don Quisando?

DON QUISANDO chuckles.

ROGER: There aren't many things Don Quisando – alias Monsieur Andrianopolis – doesn't know about Marapest.

QUISANDO: I am only too happy to be of service, senor!

LINDA: But Don Quisando – you told me in Casablanca to contact Tinker-Bell Smith – and yet when we got in touch with Smith he told me that Roger had actually visited him in order to buy the musical-box.

ROGER: I can explain. You see, when I discovered that Van Zyland couldn't be located I realised my position was a pretty dangerous one.

LINDA: Why?

ROGER: Well, it looked as if he suspected what my game was – he'd use the musical-box to trap me.

LINDA: Yes, I see.

ROGER: So just for safety I got Tinker-Bell Smith to say that I was a prospective buyer. I reckoned Van Zyland wouldn't bother so much about me – if he thought I was just after the musical-box like he was. In fact his anxiety to get in touch with me might actually bring him out of hiding.

TIM: Yes, of course. Well – then what?

ROGER: Well, naturally enough, several people – most of them quite innocent – turned up to ask about the musical-box. We'd anticipated that – and Smith ...

TIM:	Smith dished out the story about selling it to Ruby Thompson?
ROGER:	Yes. Years ago Smith met Van Zyland and I know once he showed up Tinker ...
LINDA:	But Roger, you visited Ruby Thompson yourself and asked her about the musical-box so ...
ROGER:	(*Amused*) Yes – it was an awfully good way of getting to know her!
LINDA:	(*Half annoyed, half amused*) Oh, Roger!
TIM:	But – why did you disappear so suddenly?
ROGER:	I'll tell you why, Tim! Because things began to get too hot for me! Philip Millais heard that I was after the musical-box and ...
QUISANDO:	Four attempts on your life are not exactly a joke, senor!
ROGER:	Millais was after the musical-box because he knew where Van Zyland was and he wanted to do a deal with him.
TIM:	(*Thoughtfully*) Yes. I'm just beginning to see exactly what happened. Millais thought that you were in this business for the same reason as Van Zyland – for personal gain. He was under the impression that you'd contacted your sister, with the intention of bringing her into it, just in case ...
LINDA:	Just in case something happened to Roger?
TIM:	Yes. Extraordinary! How perfectly extraordinary!
ROGER:	When I made up my mind to disappear for a little while, I knew that reports would get abroad that I'd been murdered, so I got in touch with a Canadian called Peter Vandare. I was under the impression – and still am for

	that matter – that Vandare is a member of British Intelligence. I asked him to send my watch through to Linda – I scribbled a message on the strap telling her not to worry if she didn't hear …
LINDA:	(*Interrupting ROGER*) You asked Peter Vandare to send the watch through to <u>me</u>?
ROGER:	Why, yes!
LINDA:	But the watch was sent to Major Hadley – surely, those were your instructions?
ROGER:	Major Hadley?
LINDA:	Yes.
TIM:	Major Hadley is in charge of the Foreign Investigation Branch of British Intelligence. He … (*He stops, quietly*) Roger – what exactly – was the message … you sent to Linda on the watch?
ROGER:	I simply scribbled a sentence to the effect that she wouldn't be hearing from me for some little time, and that I was perfectly all right. I sent it on the wristwatch so that she'd know it was genuine.
TIM:	Then, what does this mean – Not far from Oran there is a place called Ras-el-Ma?
ROGER:	(*Surprised*) Not far from Oran there is a place called Ras-el-Ma?
TIM:	Yes.
ROGER:	I haven't the faintest idea, old boy.
TIM:	Don Quisando?
QUISANDO:	(*Puzzled*) It does not make sense to me, senor!
LINDA:	But – but Roger – that was the message on the watch!
ROGER:	(*Staggered*) What!

QUISANDO:	Impossible, senora! Why …
TIM:	Show them the watch, Linda!

A rattle as LINDA takes the watch from her handbag.

ROGER:	(*After a moment – staggered*) But, Linda, the strap's been changed! This isn't the same strap! It's my watch all right, but – but …
TIM:	(*Tensely*) But Vandare changed the strap, changed the message, and sent the watch through to Hadley instead of Linda!
ROGER:	(*Bewildered*) He must have done.
LINDA:	(*Confused*) But Tim – what does …?
QUISANDO:	(*Quickly – astonished*) But what does this mean, senor?
TIM:	(*Tensely – dramatically*) It means, my dear Don Quisando – that Peter Vandare – is Kurt Van Zyland!
ROGER:	Good God!
QUISANDO:	But senor – Peter Vandare is a member of British Intelligence surely …
TIM:	But don't you see what happened? The real Peter Vandare is dead. Van Zyland murdered him and took his place.
LINDA:	But Tim …
TIM:	Don't you see! Vandare – or Van Zyland rather – was lying when he told us that Mrs Penelope had been murdered by Millais. You can see exactly what happened. Mrs Penelope was sent by Major Hadley to act as your – well – bodyguard. She left you at Casablanca in order not to make things look too obvious, and flew to Marapest. When she arrived at Marapest she quite naturally got in touch with Peter Vandare. She realised as soon as she met him that he was a phoney and started to

107

	keep an eye on him. She followed him to Tinker-Bell Smith's and – well …
QUISANDO:	The rest we can guess, senor.
LINDA:	But why should Vandare – or Van Zyland – change the strap on my watch and substitute an entirely ridiculous message for …?
TIM:	Because he thought Roger might have already contacted the British Intelligence people in London. So as a precaution he decided to take a chance and put them on the wrong scent. Don't you remember what he said to us this evening?
LINDA:	He said surely that message indicated that Oran should have been the real centre for investigations.
TIM:	Exactly – the wrong scent! It fits! It fits together like a jigsaw!
ROGER:	But look here, you say that you actually saw Van Zyland – tonight?
LINDA:	Yes. We met him at The Villanova. Why … (*Suddenly*) Why, I'm supposed to be having dinner with him tomorrow at The Martinique!
QUISANDO:	(*Excitedly*) Then surely, senor, this – this is your opportunity!
ROGER:	(*Tensely*) Yes! Yes! I'll surround the place! I'll have every police official in Marapest on …!
TIM:	And he'll slip through your fingers like a piece of ice! Quisando's right! This is your opportunity – but by God we've got to watch it! Now listen! Van Zyland still isn't at all certain that you're not in this business for what you can get out of it. Now I suggest that

	tomorrow night Linda, quite boldly, puts her cards on the table!
ROGER:	(*Astonished*) What!
QUISANDO:	Senor!
TIM:	She'll tell him that she's found her brother and that Roger's prepared to do a deal over the musical-box. She'll suggest that he comes back here to the El Bassari to meet Roger and – well – discuss the details.
ROGER:	(*Excitedly*) But will he fall for that?
TIM:	Why shouldn't he? You'll have to be careful, Linda – devilishly careful – but I think he'll fall for it.
ROGER:	Yes! (*Thoughtfully*) Yes, I think perhaps he will!

Music starts.

QUISANDO:	(*Delighted – chuckling*) Come into my parlour said the spider to the fly! (*He chuckles more*)

FADE UP music to full.

FADE DOWN on the last note.
A knock on a door.

LINDA:	Come in!

The door opens.

TIM:	Nearly ready?
LINDA:	Oh, hello!

The door closes.

TIM:	(*Coming in – pleasantly surprised*) My word, that's a pretty corking dress you're wearing!
LINDA:	Do you like it?
TIM:	I certainly do – it's – it's corking!
LINDA:	(*Laughing – then:*) Has he arrived yet?

TIM: Yes, he's on the terrace. I spotted him from
            my bedroom window. It's Van Zyland all
            right – Smith phoned through to my room.
            He's been watching the front entrance.

LINDA: He recognised him?

TIM: Yes. (*A moment*) Are you nervous?

LINDA: Well – just a little …

TIM: Don't worry, there won't be any funny
            business. I shall be waiting with Tinker-Bell
            Smith. As soon as you leave for the El Bassari
            we shall be on your trail.

LINDA: I'm – I'm not worried.

TIM: Good. Would you like a cocktail before you
            join him?

LINDA: No. No, I don't think so.

TIM: I say, you – you certainly look …

LINDA: Corking?

TIM and LINDA laugh.

TIM: Linda, I've – I've been meaning to say this
            for a very long time. When this business is all
            over I – I hope that …

LINDA: That what?

TIM: Well – that we shall – sort of – kind of …
            (*Laughing*) Gosh, I'm not usually tied up like
            this when I talk to a girl. (*Suddenly*) Oh, I
            don't mean that! I mean, I'm not usually sort
            of – kind of …

LINDA: (*Gently – laughing*) Come on, Tim!

TIM: (*Suddenly – seriously*) Linda, don't forget.
            Van Zyland isn't a fool – not by any stretch of
            the imagination … so …

LINDA: (*Softly*) I'll take care, darling.

FADE DOWN the last speech.

Music starts and changes to a dance tune – possibly with a vocal.

There is light applause at the end of the vocal – the music continues.

Light chatter is in the background.

VANDARE: You know, Miss West, this is an unusual situation. I came along here tonight feeling kinda lonely and despondent because – well – because I'd no news for you about your brother, and – well, lo and behold – you've actually found the guy!

The music finishes – light applause follows.

LINDA: (*Quietly*) Mr Vandare, I've had a most enjoyable evening – but don't you think – it's about time we put our cards on the table?

VANDARE: Put our cards on the table, young lady? (*Amused*) Now what exactly do you mean by that?

LINDA: What do you imagine I mean by it? I mean – how much are you prepared to pay for the musical-box?

VANDARE: For the musical-box? What musical-box? Say – say, what is this – some kind of a joke or something? You know you English always tickle me to death – you accuse us Canadians of …

LINDA: (*Interrupting VANDARE*) Mr Vandare – or perhaps I should say – Kurt Van Zyland!

A coffee cup is knocked over.

VANDARE: (*After a moment – tensely*) What does your brother want?

LINDA: For the musical-box?

VANDARE: Yes.

111

LINDA:	(*Without a moment's hesitation*) Two hundred thousand dollars!
VANDARE:	Two hundred ... (*He suddenly laughs*) Is he crazy?
LINDA:	(*Unruffled*) Two hundred thousand dollars, Van Zyland.
VANDARE:	(*Suddenly*) Where is he? Where is your brother?

Music starts.

LINDA:	You'd like to see him?
VANDARE:	Yes.
LINDA:	Tonight?
VANDARE:	Yes! Yes – tonight!
LINDA:	He's at the Café El Bassari.
VANDARE:	Café El Bassari? Where the devil's that?
LINDA:	It's in the Rue Galicia. Have you a car?
VANDARE:	Yes – it's outside on the drive.
LINDA:	(*With authority*) Good, then get your things.
VANDARE:	Just a minute – just a minute – who's giving the orders around here anyway?
LINDA:	What are you frightened of?
VANDARE:	I'm not frightened of anything, but I'm kinda careful. Kinda careful by nature. You'll maybe find that out, Miss West.
LINDA:	(*Quietly*) Get your things and meet me at the car.
VANDARE:	Yeah, yeah, O.K. (*Thoughtfully*) Café El Bassari.

FADE UP music to full, FADING DOWN the last words of above speech and FADING OUT chatter.

CROSSFADE the last note of the music with a car ticking over.

SMITH:	(*Suddenly*) There they are, guv'nor! They're just getting into the car!
TIM:	Yes. By George, she's pulled it off all right!
SMITH:	We'd better wait a minute or two.
TIM:	Yes.

The sound of Vandare's car departing in the background is heard.

SMITH:	O.K. now?
TIM:	Yes – keep close but don't get too near.

The sound in the foreground of SMITH's car making a speedy departure.

FADE OUT SMITH's car.

FADE IN VANDARE's car.

LINDA:	When you reach the river – turn right.
VANDARE:	Rue Galicia?
LINDA:	Yes.

A pause.

VANDARE:	Would you mind closing the window?
LINDA:	I – I only opened it because – because (*She is suddenly very languid*) I thought that – that …
VANDARE:	(*Quietly, watching LINDA*) You look tired.
LINDA:	Yes. Yes, I can't understand it. I – I – feel so sleepy – I …
VANDARE:	(*Chuckles – then:*) O.K. Leave it open.

Slight pause.

LINDA:	(*Bewildered, sleepy*) What is it? What's – what's the matter with me? Why should I …
VANDARE:	You'll be all right.
LINDA:	(*Alarmed*) But – but why should I feel like this. I – I … (*Suddenly, desperately attempting to pull herself together*) What is it? What's the matter with me?
VANDARE:	(*A little laugh*) You'll be O.K.

113

LINDA:	(*A moment*) Oh … Oh, my head …
VANDARE:	(*Quietly*) Lie back. Put your head on the seat.
LINDA:	I feel terrible – terrible …
VANDARE:	I've told you not to worry – you'll be perfectly all right if you just relax.
LINDA:	(*Weakly*) It was the coffee, wasn't it? You – you drugged the coffee … You – drugged – the – coffee …
VANDARE:	(*Quietly*) Just relax – take it easy. (*Chuckles*) I told you I was very careful.
LINDA:	Why did you …? (*Suddenly, desperately*) No! No! You turn right over the river! I – told – you, you … (*Weakly*) You turn – Rue Galicia … Rue – Galicia …
VANDARE:	(*Softly*) Relax.

FADE OUT VANDARE's car.

FADE IN SMITH's car.

TIM:	I say – I say, he ought to have taken <u>that</u> turning – the one on the right!
SMITH:	Yes. There's something queer going on, if you ask me! Shall I overtake him?
TIM:	Yes! Yes, you'd better! We can't take any chances!
SMITH:	Wait a minute!
TIM:	What is it?
SMITH:	He's slowing down by the look of things.
TIM:	Is there another turning? Can he …?
SMITH:	He's turning the car. I don't know what he's up to.
TIM:	(*Puzzled*) He's got something in his hand. Look – I …
SMITH:	(*Suddenly*) Look out! Look out!

A revolver shot is heard and the smashing of glass – the screeching of brakes – a second revolver shot followed by the loud explosion of a burst tyre.

SMITH: He's done it! He's hit our front tyre!!

TIM: (*Desperately*) Blast!

SMITH's car pulls up.

SMITH: Strewth!!

TIM: What are we going to do?

SMITH: (*Tensely – desperately*) We can't go on – that's a cert! We can't chase the swine with a flat tyre! Oh, strewth! This is a pretty kettle of fish and no mistake!

Music starts full up.

FADE DOWN music on the last note.

FADE IN a phoned being 'jiggled'.

ROGER: What the devil's the matter with this phone?

TIM: Roger, listen! You've got to listen! If you call in the local police now we're sunk! We're sunk – hook, line and sinker!

ROGER: Hello!

The receiver is jiggled again.

QUISANDO: He's right, senor! It will be questions – questions – nothing but questions!

The receiver is replaced with a bang.

ROGER: Tim, listen! I don't give two hoots in hell what we do! But we've got to find Linda – and we've got to find her <u>tonight</u>!

TIM: Good God, man, do you think I don't want to find her? I'd walk from here to London and back if I thought it would help matters! But losing our heads isn't going to get us anywhere.

ROGER: (*Losing his temper*) You should have stuck to the car! Flat tyre or no flat tyre you should have stuck to the car!

QUISANDO: But that was impossible, senor!

TIM: Now, Roger, listen! Pull yourself together! I know how you feel about this business and I'm sorry – desperately sorry – about what happened tonight. But – well – after all, you're only her brother – I'm the guy's that's in love with the girl!

ROGER: (*Surprised*) In love with Linda?

TIM: Don't be silly, old boy – you can't have a corny situation like this and not have someone in love with the girl! (*A moment – quietly*) Of course I'm in love with her. I think I've been in love with her from the very first moment we met. I think ... (*Suddenly, tensely*) By God, you're right! If Van Zyland so much as ...

QUISANDO: Senor, please! Please! You are both getting emotional – let us be sensible about this business! Nothing is going to happen to the senorita! You see, senor – you still have the musical-box! And the man who possesses the musical-box calls the tune! (*He chuckles*)

TIM: (*Quietly*) Yes. Yes, he's right, Roger.

ROGER: (*Distressed*) I'm sorry I lost my temper, Tim – but ...

TIM: Oh, that's all right. (*Suddenly, briskly*) Now, Quisando, you know this place – you know this island backwards – where the devil has he taken her?

QUISANDO: Senor, that is a difficult question. He might have taken the senorita to one of the many

116

villages north of the mountains, or perhaps even to ...

The telephone rings, interrupting QUISANDO. It continues to ring.

ROGER: (*After a moment*) Who's this?

QUISANDO: I don't know. Unless Tinker-Bell Smith has discovered something and ...

The receiver is lifted.

TIM: (*On the phone*) Hello? ... Hello? Who ...?

VANDARE: (*Quietly*) Good evening, Mr Valentine.

TIM: (*Suddenly, tensely*) My God! Van Zyland!

QUISANDO: (*Astonished*) Van Zyland!

ROGER: Van Zy ...! Let me talk to the ...!

TIM: (*Quickly – tensely*) Van Zyland, listen! Listen, you swine ... if you don't release Miss ...

VANDARE: (*Interrupting TIM*) Mr Valentine, I think there's a friend of yours here – who would rather like to have a word with you.

TIM: What?

LINDA is heard. She is obviously greatly distressed.

LINDA: (*Distressed*) Hello?

TIM: Linda! Linda, are you all right?

LINDA: (*Distressed, faintly hysterical*) Tim – tell Roger he's got to give – got to give the musical-box to – to Van Zyland ... Tell him – he's got to! He's got to! He's got to! (*Near hysteria*)

TIM: Linda!

Music starts.

VANDARE: Did you hear that, Mr Valentine?

TIM: (*Desperately*) Van Zyland, you swine, I'll – I'll ...

VANDARE: (*A little laugh*) You'll do precisely nothing. (*Suddenly, fiercely*) Now listen, my friend –

117

and listen carefully! These are your
instructions …

CROSSFADE the last words of speech down and music up to
full to finish.

END OF EPISODE FIVE

EPISODE SIX

IN WHICH THE YOUNG LADY SAYS "YES" AGAIN

ANNOUNCER:	During a visit to the Isle of Marapest, Roger Knight, Foreign Correspondent of The Daily Graphic, has mysteriously disappeared. His sister – Linda West, the well-known actress – flies to Marapest in the hope of discovering her brother's whereabouts. She arrives on the island, accompanied by a friend of hers – Timothy Valentine. After a series of adventures, in the course of which she succeeds in finding her brother, Linda is kidnapped by a notorious criminal known as Kurt Van Zyland. Van Zyland, who has been masquerading as Peter Vandare, a member of the British Intelligence Service, is endeavouring to gain possession of a mysterious musical-box at the moment in the hands of Roger Knight.

Music starts.

ANNOUNCER:	Tim, Roger and Don Quisando – a Spanish friend of Roger's – discuss the situation in a room at the Café el Bassari.

FADE UP music to full, then down and out under dialogue.

QUISANDO:	Senor, please! Please! You are both getting emotional – let us be sensible about this business! Nothing is going to happen to the senorita! You see, senor – you still have the musical-box! And the man who possesses the musical-box calls the tune!
TIM:	(*Quickly*) Yes. Yes, he's right, Roger.
ROGER:	(*Distressed*) I'm sorry I lost my temper, Tim – but …

TIM: Oh, that's all right. (*Suddenly, briskly*) Now, Quisando, you know this place – you know this island backwards – where the devil has he taken her?

QUISANDO: Senor, that is a difficult question. He might have taken the senorita to one of the many villages north of the mountains, or perhaps even to ...

The telephone rings.

ROGER: Who's this?

QUISANDO: I don't know. Unless Tinker-Bell Smith has discovered something and ...

The receiver is lifted.

TIM: (*On the phone*) Hello? ... Hello? Who ...?

VANDARE: (*Quietly*) Good evening, Mr Valentine.

TIM: (*Suddenly, tensely*) My God! Van Zyland!

QUISANDO: (*Astonished*) Van Zyland!

ROGER: Van Zy ...! Let me talk to the ...!

TIM: (*Quickly – tensely*) Van Zyland, listen! Listen, you swine ... if you don't release Miss ...

VANDARE: (*Interrupting TIM*) Mr Valentine, I think there's a friend of yours here – who would rather like to have a word with you.

TIM: What?

LINDA: (*Distressed*) Hello?

TIM: Linda! Linda, are you all right?

LINDA: (*Distressed, faintly hysterical*) Tim – tell Roger he's got to give – got to give the musical-box to – to Van Zyland ... Tell him – he's got to! He's got to! He's got to! (*Near hysteria*)

TIM: Linda!

VANDARE: Did you hear that, Mr Valentine?

122

TIM:	(*Desperately*) Van Zyland, you swine, I'll – I'll …
VANDARE:	(*A little laugh*) You'll do precisely nothing. (*Suddenly, fiercely*) Now listen, my friend – and listen carefully! These are your instructions: Tell your friend Roger Knight to bring the musical-box to the following address – 842 Rue Reidlinger. There is a girl at the house called Maxime – she will be waiting. If the musical-box is handed over, Miss West will be returned to the Café El Bassari by midnight. Did you get the address?
TIM:	(*After a moment – quietly*) 842 Rue Reidlinger.
VANDARE:	Yes. Now don't forget. And tell your friend – if he takes my advice, there will be no funny business.

A muffled click as the receiver is replaced.

ROGER:	(*Tensely*) Well – what did he say?
QUISANDO:	(*Anxiously*) What did he say, senor?
TIM:	(*Quietly*) He wants the musical-box – he wants Roger to deliver it to 842 Rue Reidlinger.
ROGER:	And Linda? What about Linda?
TIM:	If you deliver the musical-box … (*He pauses*)
QUISANDO:	(*Ominously*) The senorita will be returned – here – to the El Bassari?
TIM:	Yes.
ROGER:	(*Desperately*) What are we going to do? What the devil are we going to do?
QUISANDO:	Senor, suppose we take a chance tonight and raid this house – this house in the Rue Reidlinger.

TIM:	No! Van Zyland isn't at the house – or Linda for that matter – otherwise he would never have given us the address. The house is just a go between. Now if …
QUISANDO:	(*Suddenly, thoughtfully*) Senor! Senor, that telephone call …
TIM:	What about it?
QUISANDO:	If we could trace that telephone call – then …
ROGER:	Trace a telephone call? In Marapest? If you get two right numbers out of fifty it's a miracle!
QUISANDO:	Wait, senor. Wait – do not be impatient!

The receiver is lifted.

QUISANDO:	Hello? … Hello? …
OPERATOR:	Number please.
QUISANDO:	(Pleasantly) Operator, this is Don Quisando. Tell me, is my charming young friend on duty tonight? Senorita Rosita Penerando?
OPERATOR:	You wish to speak to her?
QUISANDO:	Yes – if you would be so kind!
ROSITA:	Hello.
QUISANDO:	(*A moment, suddenly very gay*) Hello! How are you, my beautiful rose? You sound so gay!
ROSITA:	What do you want?
QUISANDO:	Listen, my lovely one – you will do a little favour for Don Quisando – yes?
ROSITA:	That depends.
QUISANDO:	Just a little – little favour.
ROSITA:	You're always asking favours.
QUISANDO:	Now Rosita, don't be stupid!
ROSITA:	Well, what is it?
QUISANDO:	Well, my sweetheart – just a few moments ago we received a telephone call here at the

	El Bassari – and we have forgotten the number. Could you be so clever Rosita and find it for us?
ROSITA:	The call was to the El Bassari?
QUISANDO:	Yes, that is right, senorita.
ROSITA:	Hold the line.
ROGER:	(*After a moment – tensely*) Well?
QUISANDO:	Sh! It will be all right. (*On the phone*) Hello? …
ROSITA:	The call was on a private line.
QUISANDO:	A private line? But, Rosita, you can find out the number for me – for your Don Quisando!
ROSITA:	I don't think I can.
QUISANDO:	Yes you can, my beautiful rose!
ROSITA:	You want it now?
QUISANDO:	Of course!
ROSITA:	Just a minute, then … Are you ready?
QUISANDO:	(*A pause*) Yes?
ROSITA:	The call was from Marapest 9 – 8784.
QUISANDO:	Marapest 9 – 8784. (*Puzzled*) What is that number, Rosita?
ROSITA:	The Villa San Leandro.
QUISANDO:	The Villa San Leandro? Where is that?
ROSITA:	It's the café up in the hills.
QUISANDO:	(*Suddenly*) Oh! Oh, of course! I know! Thank you – thank you my beautiful one! Gracias!

The receiver is replaced.

QUISANDO:	Tch! She is so ugly!
TIM:	(*Quickly*) Well?
QUISANDO:	Van Zyland was telephoning from the Villa San Leandro – that's in the mountains about twenty miles north of the city.
ROGER:	Villa San Leandro?

QUISANDO: Yes. You know the place – large open café with an orchestra and dancing – always they have a sort of fiesta.

TIM: Who owns it?

QUISANDO: A woman called Tressburg – Mrs Strachen Tressburg.

Music starts.

TIM: Get the car, Roger! Quisando, get Tinker-Bell Smith – we need all the help we can get!

QUISANDO: (*Excitedly*) Si, senor – si!

Quickly FADE UP music.

CROSSFADE music down and a car starting off quickly.

CROSSFADE the car out and music up to full.

FADE DOWN music on the last note.

A door opens.

VANDARE: Well – are you feeling any better?

LINDA: How long are you going to keep me here?

VANDARE: That depends. That depends entirely upon whether your brother is stupid – or …

LINDA: (*Angrily*) Van Zyland – you don't really think you're going to get away with this, do you? You don't really think …

VANDARE: (*Acidly*) I think it would be wiser of you, Miss West, if you started to realise that you're in a pretty serious situation.

LINDA starts to laugh.

VANDARE: Why are you laughing? (*Furiously*) Why are you laughing?

LINDA: I'm laughing at your conceit! Your stupidity! Your …

126

VANDARE:	(*Interrupting LINDA*) Miss West – I have invited your brother to visit a certain house in the Rue Reidlinger. If he chooses to ignore my request ...
LINDA:	There will be dirty work at the crossroads! Van Zyland, take a look at yourself! Take a look at yourself! You look just like the villain out of Scene 3 Act 2!

VANDARE slaps LINDA's face.

LINDA:	Why you – you swine! You filthy swine! (*Near to tears*)
VANDARE:	(*A chuckle*) Excellent! Excellent! Now you're running true to form also, Miss West – and I much prefer it!

A door opens.

VANDARE:	(*Sharply*) What do you want?
TRESSBURG:	(*A woman of about 50 – nervous and with a foreign accent*) Have you telephoned?
VANDARE:	Yes. Tell Maxime to get down to the house – and warn her that she might be followed on her way back. Have Strachen and Carl ready – just in case.
TRESSBURG:	You think he'll deliver the musical-box?
VANDARE:	Yes. But Maxime mustn't be followed – you understand – that's most important!
TRESSBURG:	Don't worry – if anyone follows her from the Rue Reidlinger they won't get further than the Place Ferdinando. Strachen will see to that all right.
VANDARE:	Good.
TRESSBURG:	Are you coming downstairs tonight – there is a fiesta and Renee is going to sing.
VANDARE:	No. No, I think I shall wait in my room. Send Maxime to me as soon as she arrives.

TRESSBURG: Yes. (*A moment*) Van Zyland – you know what you promised.

VANDARE: Yes – and if the musical-box is delivered I shall keep my word, Mrs Tressburg.

TRESSBURG: 10,000 dollars.

VANDARE: 10,000 dollars.

TRESSBURG: (*Slowly*) That musical-box must be worth – quite a lot of money, my friend.

VANDARE: To you, my dear Mrs Tressburg, 10,000 dollars!

Music starts.

TRESSBURG: (*A moment, she suddenly chuckles*) I shall see you later.

Quickly FADE UP music.

FADE music down, fading in the sound of a car arriving and pulling up.
The music changes to a dance tune.
FADE IN a background of chatter and laughter.

The car door opens.

TIM: Is this the only entrance to this place?

QUISANDO: Yes. Yes, I think so, senor.

The car door closes.

SMITH: One of us 'ad better stay with the car! If there's any funny business we don't want to dash out an' find the ruddy engine smashed to bits.

ROGER: I think you're right.

TIM: You stay here, Tinker-Bell – if you need any help just …

SMITH: I shan't need any help. – don't worry about that.

TIM: O.K. Roger?

ROGER: Yes – I'm ready.

QUISANDO: That's the Villa, senor – they use the grounds as the restaurant. Quite a paying proposition they tell me – the Villa San Leandro.

Slowly FADE UP music and chatter a little.

JACQUES: (*A Frenchman about thirty-six – coming in*) Good evening, gentlemen.

TIM: Good evening – we'd like a table for three, please.

JACQUES: (*A little laugh*) Oh, monsieur! I am so sorry! There is not a table left to offer you – everywhere it is absolutely full. Tonight, you see, Renee is singing. It is a fiesta – and …

QUISANDO: And we should like a table, my friend! A table for three.

JACQUES: Monsieur, I am desolate, but I cannot …

QUISANDO: I am a personal friend of Mrs Tressburg – if you mention my name – Don Quisando – I feel sure …

JACQUES: Ah, well – in that case, senior – this way if you please.

FADE UP music, which finishes.

There is applause followed by laughter and chatter.

JACQUES: This is the best table I can offer you, gentlemen. I am so sorry, but …

ROGER: This will do quite nicely, thank you.

JACQUES: I'll tell the waiter to take your order in just a few moments.

ROGER: Thank you.

QUISANDO: (*After a moment*) It's a big place, senor – a lot could happen here without one knowing.

TIM: Yes. (*Quietly*) Stay here, Roger – I'm going to have a look round.

ROGER: Watch yourself!

129

QUISANDO: (*A warning*) Careful, senor!

TIM: (*Going*) Don't worry.

There is a cymbal roll. The chatter and laughter dies down.

DUMAS: (*Away – announcing*) Mesdames and messieurs – tonight I have great pleasure in welcoming back to the Villa San Leandro your friend – my friend – everybody's friend – Renee!

There is applause, laughter and cheers.

RENEE and the orchestra perform Darling, Je Vous Aime Beaucoup.

During the song, slowly FADE DOWN the singing voice and orchestra for dialogue.

A door opens.

TRESSBURG: (*Coming in*) Are you looking for something, monsieur?

TIM: (*Startled*) Oh! Oh, I'm sorry. I thought this was the way to the restaurant. (*A friendly little laugh*) I seem to have got lost, I'm afraid.

TRESSBURG: (*Quietly, watching TIM*) Through the tropical garden, monsieur – on the left.

TIM: How extraordinary! How perfectly extraordinary! I've just come from there.

TRESSBURG: Then you should find your way back quite easily, monsieur.

TIM: (*A laugh*) Er – yes – yes.

Slowly FADE UP the orchestra and singing voice. The song finishes and is followed by applause, shouts of Bravo, etc, dying down to general chatter and laughter.

ROGER: (*Quietly, tensely*) Well?

QUISANDO: What did you find, senor?

TIM:	Nothing. It's a pretty big place, this – it stretches a devil of a way. There must be twenty or thirty rooms in the Villa.
QUISANDO:	Did you see anyone?
TIM:	Yes – I tried to get in, but bumped bang-slap into an old dame with jet-black hair. Would that be Mrs Tressburg?
QUISANDO:	Yes.
TIM:	She looks a pretty tough customer to me.
QUISANDO:	She wants watching, senor.
ROGER:	Look here, what are we going to do? We can't just sit here and order dinner. If Linda's here at the Villa – then obviously …
TIM:	Then obviously we must watch our step and act at the right time. If we do anything on the spur of the moment we shall regret it.
QUISANDO:	You are right, senor. There is always a time to wait and a time to act. At the moment – we wait!
TIM:	(*After a moment*) You've been here before, Quisando?
QUISANDO:	Once or twice, senor – a long time ago.
TIM:	What happens? Do the people get noisy – gay – out of hand?
QUISANDO:	Later in the evening, senor, they perhaps get a little gay, noisy – sometimes there are a few fireworks. It is always – what do you say? – very jolly.

Music starts.

TIM:	And sometimes rather boisterous, perhaps?
QUISANDO:	Si, si, senor – sometimes.
TIM:	(*Quietly, urgently*) Good. Then I suggest we wait until things get hotted up – and then …
ROGER:	(*Softly, a warning*) Sh! Here's the waiter!

QUISANDO: (*Brightly, for the waiter's benefit*) They serve a shell fish here, senor, that is absolutely delightful. They are a little fish with blue claws and in appearance they are not entirely unlike ...

FADE UP music to full, fading out chatter and laughter.

FADE DOWN music on the last note.

FADE IN the tapping of a typewriter.
A door opens. The typewriter stops.
VANDARE: (*Impatiently*) What is it?
The door closes.
TRESSBURG: (*Coming in – nervously*) Van Zyland – that man – the one you spoke to on the telephone ...
VANDARE: You mean Valentine – Timothy Valentine?
TRESSBURG: Yes.
VANDARE: Well? (*A moment*) Well, what is it?
TRESSBURG: He's here – at the Villa.
VANDARE: (*Sharply*) What!
TRESSBURG: There are two other men with him – you can see them if you look out of the window – they're over on the far side – (*A pause*) Well – do you see them?
VANDARE: (*Angrily*) How the devil! ... You fool! You damned fool! I asked you if that telephone was a private line, and ...
TRESSBURG: It is a private line! They couldn't have traced ...
VANDARE: They must have traced it! (*Quickly, tensely*) Does the girl know they're here?
TRESSBURG: No, of course not.
VANDARE: Can she see them from her window?

132

TRESSBURG: No. (*A pause*) What are you going to do?

VANDARE: There's only one thing I can do. I've got to get the girl away from here – quickly – damned quickly! Has Strachen left for the Rue Reidlinger?

TRESSBURG: He left about half an hour ago with Carl.

VANDARE: Ach!

TRESSBURG: You can't leave without taking the girl through the restaurant.

VANDARE: Then I'll have to risk it!

TRESSBURG: Well – listen! I'll tell Dumas to play a czardas – that always gets the people excited – the dance floor should be crowded. While the people are dancing you can take the girl across the floor and out through the main entrance. I'll have the car ready.

VANDARE: (*A moment's hesitation*) Yes. Yes, all right.

TRESSBURG: Take her to the chalet – you know the place I mean – not far from the San Leandro Bridge. Then tomorrow, if you like, you can bring her back to the Villa.

VANDARE: Yes. I'll go upstairs and talk to the girl now.

TRESSBURG: Don't leave until the people are pretty excited, and there's plenty of dancing.

VANDARE: Dim the lights if you can.

TRESSBURG: You'll get through if you can keep the girl quiet!

VANDARE: Don't worry about that.

TRESSBURG: Phone me when you get to the chalet.

VANDARE: Yes.

Music starts full up.

FADE DOWN on the last note.
A key is placed in a lock – the door is unlocked and opens.

133

LINDA:	(*Tensely*) Leave me alone! Get out! Please – please leave me alone!
VANDARE:	(*Quietly, much more pleasant*) Miss West, I'm awfully sorry to disturb you, but something rather important has happened – rather important to me, that is.
LINDA:	(*Coming in*) Well?
VANDARE:	Well, you know that I had arranged that you should be returned to the Café El Bassari immediately your brother ...
LINDA:	Immediately Roger handed over the musical-box.
VANDARE:	Yes.
LINDA:	Well?
VANDARE:	Well – your brother seems to have changed his mind.
LINDA:	(*Frightened*) What do you mean?
VANDARE:	Your brother now insists that before he hands over the musical-box you should be – well – handed over to our mutual friend Mr Valentine.
LINDA:	(*Relieved*) Oh!
VANDARE:	I have, unfortunately, no alternative but to accept the proposition.
LINDA:	You mean ...?
VANDARE:	I mean, that at this very moment, Mr Valentine is waiting for you at The Martinique. I have agreed to take you there – on one condition.
LINDA:	What is it?
VANDARE:	That you give me your word of honour that under no circumstances will you try to escape, or even attract attention to yourself. When we arrive at the hotel you will be quite at liberty

to leave the car and join Mr Valentine. I shall then proceed to the Café El Bassari where your brother has promised to hand over the musical-box. (*A moment*) Have I your word of honour under no circumstances ...?

Music starts – not faded up.

LINDA: (*Tensely, excited*) Yes! Yes, of course! Of course!

VANDARE: Thank you. We shall leave in about ten minutes.

FADE DOWN during the last speech.

FADE IN music, with much laughter and chatter. If possible, the sound of Chinese crackers exploding.

ROGER: Hello – they've put the lights out!

QUISANDO: They're going to light the lanterns.

TIM: (*Suspiciously*) All very pretty-pretty. A bit too pretty if you ask me!

ROGER: What do you mean?

TIM: Things have livened up a bit too quickly for my liking – I'm not so sure there isn't something behind all this.

QUISANDO: Si, senor – I agree – it looks very suspicious.

The music finishes. There is high-spirited applause and laughter.

ROGER: (*Impatiently*) Well – what do you propose we do? We can't just sit here and do nothing!

TIM: No – we'll give them another five minutes and then have a crack at it. You know what to do, Quisando?

QUISANDO: Sure. I'm ver – very drunk, senor. Very drunk – very happy. I wander into the Villa, I'm – I'm so drunk. I don't know what I'm doing or – hic! – where I'm going!

135

There is a cymbal roll followed by laughter and applause.

TIM: Good. Now after Quisando's disappearance, Roger, I want you to ... (*Stops, surprised*) Hello! What's this?

DUMAS: (*Announcing gaily*) Mesdames et messieurs – ladies and gentlemen – senors et senoras. (*Laughter*) Tonight for the best czardas – a bottle of champagne!

There is laughter and applause.

The orchestra starts. During the music there is considerable laughter and excitement.

At the peak of the excitement, in the mid-distance, a shot is heard followed by angry shots and the sound of a car departing quickly.

ROGER: Did you hear that?

TIM: What the devil ...? What's this? ... Smith! He's pushing his way through the ...

QUISANDO: (*Startled*) Senor!

There are lots of angry voices.

QUISANDO: (*Alarmed*) Senor! Senor, he's been shot!

A woman shrieks.

The music peters out as the crowd chatter excitedly.

TIM: What is it? Smith, what is it?

ROGER: Tinker, what happened?

SMITH: (*Gasping*) He's – taken – the girl! I tried to stop him, but – I tried to stop him but – Van Zyland shot – shot ...

TIM: (*Quickly, tensely*) Which way have they gone?

ROGER: Tinker – which way have they gone?

SMITH: Towards – towards the bridge ...

SMITH collapses and crashes across the table, knocking over a chair and some bottles. A woman shrieks.

TIM: (*Excitedly*) Stay with Smith, Quisando! Roger, come on! Come on!

The music starts full up.
FADE OUT chatter, etc.

FADE DOWN music.
FADE IN TIM's car going fast.

ROGER: (*Excited*) There's a car, Tim – there's a car!
TIM: D'you think it's them?
ROGER: It's got to be! Step on it, Tim – step on it!
CROSSFADE music up to full with TIM's car fading out.

CROSSFADE VANDARE's car in and the music out.

LINDA: (*Tensely*) Stop the car! Stop the car!
VANDARE: (*Desperately*) Keep your hands off the wheel! Keep your blasted …
LINDA: I warn you, if you don't stop I shall …
VANDARE: Keep your hands off the wheel!
LINDA: (*Slowly, threatening VANDARE*) Now listen! This is your last chance! If you don't!
VANDARE: We're near the bridge! If you touch the wheel now, I'll – I'll …!
LINDA: (*Desperately*) Van Zyland, listen to me! I warn you it's your last chance!
VANDARE: Keep your … (*Suddenly, tensely*) You fool!
The car skids.
VANDARE: You fool – you damned young …
LINDA screams.
The car hits a parapet and crashes.
TIM's car arrives and pulls up sharply.
A car door opens.
TIM: Linda! Linda!
ROGER: Oh, my …!

TIM: (*Quickly*) There she is – over on the bank! She must have been thrown out of the car!

ROGER: Linda! Linda!

FADE OUT.

FADE IN.

TIM: (*Anxiously*) Is she all right?

ROGER: She's fainted – but I think she'll be all right ...

TIM: Her shoulder seems to be hurt. There's a hospital about a quarter of a mile back.

ROGER: Yes, I noticed it.

TIM: We'd better take her there, Roger – I'll turn the car round.

ROGER: What about Van Zyland?

TIM: He's dead. He was trapped in his seat.

ROGER: Have you searched him?

TIM: Yes. I've got the paper you want and his wallet.

ROGER: Good. We'll sort them out in the car.

LINDA: (*Softly*) My shoulder – it's – terribly painful.

ROGER: Yes – but you're all right, Linda, thank God.

LINDA: I – I suppose I had a – lucky escape.

ROGER: I'll say you did.

Music starts.

TIM: How extraordinary! Perfectly extraordinary.

FADE UP music, fading down the last speech.

FADE DOWN the last note of the music, FADING IN speech.

NURSE: Now you mustn't stay very long, monsieur – mademoiselle is still very tired.

TIM: I just want to pop in and say "Hello", nurse – I shan't be two minutes.

NURSE: Well – only two minutes, monsieur.

A door opens and closes.

TIM: (*Almost a whisper*) Hello.

LINDA:	Hello.
TIM:	How are you feeling?
LINDA:	Oh, I'm fine – much better.
TIM:	Good. I've brought you some flowers.
LINDA:	Oh. Oh, thanks.
TIM:	(*A moment, nervously*) I – thought you might like some flowers.
LINDA:	They're very lovely. (*Pause*) Sit down.
TIM:	No. No, I can't stay very long, I – I can't stay very long.
LINDA:	When are you going back?
TIM:	Home?
LINDA:	Yes.
TIM:	Well, I don't know, you see ... (*Suddenly*) Well – I'm not supposed to tell this to anyone, but your great white chief has been in touch with me.
LINDA:	Who? Not – not Major Hadley?
TIM:	Yes. He wants me to go to Salzenhoff.
LINDA:	Salzenhoff? Why that's in Austria!
TIM:	Yes. You see, the Kyfhausser plan is complete now. When your brother searched Van Zyland he found the first part of the plan which was originally Kyfhausser's – and ...
LINDA:	The one all the excitement was about!
TIM:	Yes – and also the second part – the one Kyfhausser gave Van Zyland in the first place.
LINDA:	So now the British Government know ...
TIM:	Know exactly where the jewels are – yes.
LINDA:	Five hundred thousand pounds worth. It takes your breath away – doesn't it?
TIM:	Yes. Five hundred thousand pounds worth hidden in Salzenhoff.
LINDA:	(*Surprised*) In Salzenhoff?
TIM:	Yes.

LINDA: So that's why you're going there – actually to – to get the jewels?

TIM: It's a sort of special mission. Not that anything very exciting is likely to happen – it's just a question of 'collecting' as the saying goes. Still, I'm awfully glad I don't have to leave Marapest – just yet at any rate.

LINDA: Why?

TIM: Why? Well – because (*Suddenly*) I say, look here, I've been meaning to ask you this for days. Linda, are you engaged – or anything?

LINDA: No. No, I'm not engaged – or anything.

TIM: Well – are you sort of – kind of – well – so terribly wrapped up in the theatre that you'd never want to get engaged – or anything?

LINDA: I don't think I shall ever really be intrigued by the possibility of 'or anything', or even getting engaged for that matter, but …

TIM: Oh …

LINDA: But, of course, if you were to ask me to marry you, I mean straight away – this week. Tomorrow. This afternoon even, then …

TIM: Then what?

LINDA: Then I think I should say – yes please, Timothy – thank you very much.

Music starts.

TIM: (*Quietly, stunned*) Yes, please, Timothy – thank you very … (*Suddenly*) You mean … I say! I say, are you … serious?

LINDA: (*Laughing*) Of course I'm serious!

TIM: Well, I … How extraordinary! How perfectly extraordinary!

LINDA laughs. TIM joins in.
FADE UP music, fading out laughter.

FADE UP music full to the finish.

THE END

www.ingramcontent.com/pod-product-compliance
Lightning Source LLC
Chambersburg PA
CBHW022132170626
46808CB00002B/962